Impossible Things

Impossible Things

Virginia Layefsky

MARSHALL CAVENDISH ▸ NEW YORK

Library of Congress Cataloging-in-Publication Data
Layefsky, Virginia.
Impossible things / Virginia Layefsky.
p.   cm.
Summary: On his twelfth birthday, Brady discovers an unusual egg in his own
private cave on the beach near his house, and the creature that hatches from it helps
him deal with his mother's death and his father's impending remarriage.
ISBN 0-7614-5038-6
[1. Death—Fiction. 2. Fathers and sons—Fiction. 3. Mothers and sons—Fiction. 4.
Supernatural—Fiction.] I. Title.
PZ7.L4463Im   1998 [Fic]—dc21   98-11459   CIP   AC

The text of this book is set in 12 point Simoncini Garamond.

Book design by Constance Ftera

Printed in the United States of America

1   3   5   6   4   2

For everyone,
but especially Elena, Cammie, Joe, James,
and Frank Farmer—extraordinary seaman

Contents

Impossible Things

1
My Bad-Luck Birthday

My eleventh birthday was pretty good, but this last one, my twelfth, except for one unbelievably fantastic thing that happened sort of late in the day, was truly terrible from start to finish.

In the first place, it rained all day with sudden squalls, just because Stan—that's my dad—had promised me a month ago we'd go sailing on my birthday. We have this sailboat. She's named *Beruthiel*, which was the name of the queen of the cats in some story Stan likes. Don't ask me why she was named after a cat. I'd have named her *Phantom* or *Black Death* or something good anyway, but I wasn't asked. Stan named her. He probably called her that because he's a writer and writers always name their kids and boats weird things. I'm lucky he just called me Brady. He could've named me Voltaire. Knowing Stan, I guess he just didn't think of it. He's pretty weird at times. He's what is called a serious writer. That means he gets lots of letters from editors who say they admire his work and everything but can't buy it. He works pretty hard at writing, but we live on the money he makes being a handyman. Stan can fix anything, even boats. That's how we got *Beruthiel*.

Anyway, I didn't go crazy or anything when we couldn't go sailing. You can't control the weather. Besides, I still had three pretty good things to look forward to that day. One was *Star Trek*, my favorite show, that was coming on at five. It was a rerun of course, but I didn't care. You know the one where the aliens are all dressed up like ancient Romans and are into mind control? And they get Spock and Captain Kirk up on this stage and make them fight? I was hoping that one would be on that day because it's one of the ones I like best.

I had big plans for that hour. They were sort of retarded, but I was looking forward to them just the same. What I was going to do was pile up all the cushions from the couch on the floor in front of the tube to lie on while I watched and break open the bag of barbecue potato chips that I'd been saving for the right program at the right time.

The second thing was after *Star Trek* Stan and I were going to this big kind of super diner called Fat George's. Fat George's features the Mastodon. That's a triple-decker with everything on it and all the fries you can eat. What they call "the bottomless fry."

It's nice. There's this huge table in the middle of the room covered with dishes of stuff to pile on your burger, like tomatoes, lettuce, onions, cheese, bacon, mushrooms, peppers, chili sauce—you name it. It's neat. You'd like it there. You can make your own sundaes, too. Fat

George's has over twenty-seven different flavors of ice cream and twelve different toppings. And there are those real big booths with lots of light and plenty of room to sit in, and there's a video-game room right off the dining room. It's my favorite place to eat. In fact, it's the only restaurant I like at all. Did I tell you you get all the fries you can eat *automatically* at Fat George's?

Stan hadn't actually said so, but besides the Mastodons and the video games, I was pretty sure Fat George's was where he'd hand over my birthday present. It figured.

I wanted a VCR, but I knew I wouldn't get one. They're too expensive. Still, I am Stan's only kid and he always gives me something really decent for my birthday. So that was the third good thing I had to look forward to. The way it turned out, though, I lost everything. The works. *Star Trek*, Fat George's, and all.

It happened this way: there I was at five o'clock promptly in front of the tube, bag of barbecue potato chips open, hand poised to dig in at the first note of the *Star Trek* theme, and what happened? You won't believe this. The sadist who runs the station had changed the program without warning. What came on at five was an ice hockey game between Seattle and Montreal. No explanation, nothing. Combined with rain and not being able to go sailing, that's the sort of thing that can destroy you. I didn't feel too bad, though—yet. I still thought I had going to Fat George's and getting my present to look forward to. So I wasn't depressed or anything. Just sort of mad and disappointed. That was when the phone rang.

Stan was supposed to be writing, though I hadn't heard a lot of typing that afternoon, so I got up to answer it. I already had my hand on the phone, in fact, when he came charging out, falling over himself with eagerness, yelling, "I'll get it," as he practically knocked me over grabbing for it. I could tell by the way he acted he and Troy had probably had another fight and he hoped it was her calling.

Troy was Stan's steady "ghoul fiend" as my friend Harold Le Moin would say. Harold can be a real goof sometimes, but I like him. He's my best friend. We hang out together a lot. Only I don't want to talk about him right now because I was talking about Troy.

She wasn't Stan's only girl. There were others he went out with who were just girls who looked so good in tight jeans that nobody cared how much wind whistled through the vacant space between their ears. Girls like Julie and Pat. But Troy was the one he liked best. She was different from the others. She never wore jeans, forget about tight ones, and she had the right to call herself Dr. Strawbridge because Strawbridge was her last name and she had this Ph.D. in psychology. She was super intelligent: as smart as Stan and maybe smarter. She wasn't ugly or anything either. At least, her face was okay. In fact, I guess she was pretty good-looking altogether, because people were always falling in love with her and everything. Then she'd tell Stan, which usually ruined his day because they were always people who were more important than he was and didn't have two jobs like Stan did and could pay a lot of attention to her.

She also made a lot more money than Stan. She really raked in the loot. What she did was teach people how to die. That's what she did for a living.

You probably think people just go ahead and die if that's what they have to do. That's what I thought, anyway. But that's not the way it is at all. Maybe people who can't afford it just go ahead and do it—die, I mean—but people who can afford to get trained how to do it, just like people get trained to be married or to take care of babies: by an expert like old Troy.

What she did was go see people who were getting ready to die and sort of get them used to the idea. They talked to her about how they felt and everything, and then she talked back to them the stuff they were supposed to know. She said most of them wouldn't believe they were really going to die at first, and that this was normal—only it wasn't realistic or right or anything. So what she did was, she made them understand they were going to do it all right. And then, after she convinced them they were really going to die and all, she trained them to get used to the idea and be cheerful about it and not bother anybody else too much. She trained the relatives of the people who were dying to get used to the idea, too. I bet it was a lot easier for them to be cheerful about it than the ones who were really going to kick the bucket.

Anyway, that was what she did. But she didn't do it for nothing. She charged them for all that training, and if you judged by the stuff she owned, she made out like a bandit. She had money in the bank, not just sometimes, like Stan and me, but all the time. She drove a BMW, she talked about buying a boat and a condo, and she had this cat she'd paid a ton of money for.

His name was Ivan the Terrible: Ivan because old Troy wanted everyone to know he was a Russian blue—which is a very expensive kind of cat—and "the Terrible" because he was mean clear through and rotten to the core. He hissed if you practically came into the same room with him and made it pretty clear that what he would have liked to do was slash everybody in the world with his claws. Only he couldn't. He was really pretty helpless because old Troy had had all his claws pulled out. She said he was neurotic. He probably was. She ought to know.

I never liked Ivan for one instant, but sometimes I thought old Troy wasn't too bad. She was a really good cook. And she helped Stan do a lot of stuff he was really bad at, like finding stuff he'd lost and reminding him to pay bills. She was good at stuff like that. She was systematic. And she knew a lot, too. She'd read about a million books.

I don't know what she saw in Stan, except she thought he had a Big Talent and would be an important writer some day. I thought maybe that was why Stan liked her so much: because she thought that. Otherwise, I couldn't see what he saw in her, either. As I said, she knew a lot, but it was all stuff anybody could learn if they wanted to.

And she hardly ever laughed. She never thought stuff was funny. If you told her a joke she never even got it until you explained, and then she usually said something like, "What was so funny about that?" I guess Stan didn't have too much trouble listening to her tell him what a big genius he was or letting her find stuff he'd lost and didn't want to bother to look for himself, though.

"City Morgue," Stan said. He has this very terrible sense of humor when he's uneasy. Then he smiled at the phone. He has this terrifically nice smile that makes you want to do things for him and get to know him better. He also has an intelligent expression and most of his hair. The rest of him is ordinary. Women seemed to like him, though. At least, they called him up enough.

"Oh, it's you," he said. And I knew it was Troy. Even if they fought a lot, he had this special voice for her.

He went into this long routine—all nos and yeses and I-can-explains. I could tell whatever it was, they were making up. But I wasn't too interested until I heard Stan say, "Oh, not tonight, though. It's Brady's birthday and I promised to take him to Fat George's. I said, Fat George's. That's right, and I can't just . . . oh, come on, Troy, don't be such a—"

Then he shut up and listened with this pained expression. When she stopped talking, he said, "Well, maybe it's not, but he likes it there and after all, it's his birth—"

More talk from the other end.

Then Stan said, "Yeah, sure, you're probably right, but you see, I promised—" I could tell he thought I might be listening, "And anyway, we could—no, I meant later—well, if you want to know, I think you're being somewhat unreason—I can't just break a—"

But then his face lit up.

"Hey," he said, "I have a great idea. Why don't we all have dinner? I know . . . I know it's noisy there, with the video games and all, but you see, Brady—"

I listened more carefully when I heard how the conversation was going. And when I saw what was starting to happen, a big knot began to form in the place where I'd planned to put a couple of Mastodons later on, with a lump in my throat to match.

"I realize Fat George's isn't exactly your idea of—and it's not my idea of—" Stan the Rat said as he calmly invited her to my party. "But if you could overlook the food—"

I scowled at Stan, who could put away two Mastodons and a mountain of fries as fast as the next one. I wanted to yell at him, "Fat George's isn't your idea of what?" I wanted to ask him, "Since when did you stop liking it there?"

I couldn't hear what old Troy said when she interrupted him there, but I knew what she was doing all right. What she was doing was demolishing the rest of my birthday, kicking it down and stomping it out of shape like some sand castle she found on the beach. In my mind I put her on a sand dune looking out to sea while a man-eating monster with fangs a foot long crept up behind her ready to attack. But it didn't make me feel any better.

I heard Stan say doubtfully, "He likes ravioli but—I don't know—well, he might. I could ask. Oh, sure, I know what you mean. Fat George's is quite—yes, that sort of says it all. If you put it that way, what can I say?" Stan the Rat said into the phone as he rolled his eyes helplessly to the ceiling. Then, briskly, "Right. Okay. I'll ask him."

As he said good-bye I made the monster stand over old Troy—that is, what was left of her. He was crunching a bone.

"That was Troy," Stan said. He looked uncomfortable.

"So?" I said, very cold and dignified, not about to help him out.

"She'd like to have dinner with us tonight," he said, as if I'd been deaf all along. "If you wouldn't mind."

He was being all humble and polite. You could tell he was nervous and sort of sorry for what he was doing, but there went my birthday, all the same. I gave my shortest, most contemptuous laugh.

"I thought Fat George's wasn't exactly her—"

Stan really looked uncomfortable then. He was sweating it out because he thought I hadn't plumbed the depths of his rathood yet.

"Actually, to tell the truth," he said with this sort of silly look he gets sometimes, "she thought we might like to try Luigi's for a change. They make their own ravioli and everything."

Luigi's is this Italian restaurant about a mile and a half from where we live. It has candles stuck in wine bottles and a lot of little tables jammed in so close together in the dark that you can stick your elbow in some total stranger's spaghetti sauce without even leaning back in your chair. I went there once with Stan and this girl Michelle. They drank a bottle of wine and stared into each other's eyes while they talked about themselves. I don't mean to say they completely ignored me or anything, but mostly I just sat and ate the ravioli—which wasn't all that great, by the way—and then just waited around for about ten years until they were ready to go.

"The ravioli is really good," Stan said. He gave me this big, bright smile parents always give you when they're trying to get you to do something they know you don't want to do, but they do. "Okay?"

All day I'd been picturing to myself how it would be with Stan and me at Fat George's. How we'd play the video games (and I'd outscore him), how we'd sit facing each other over our Mastodons and fries in one of those big booths. Stan would listen while I told him, scene by scene, with dialogue and all, this cool film I'd seen called *The Incredible Shrinking Man*. Stan likes me to tell him stuff like that. How we'd be alone together and things would be a little bit the way they used to be.

"By the way," Stan said, "happy birthday."

"By the way," I said, "where's my present?" I just wanted to check it out and be sure my birthday really was going to be as rotten as I thought.

"Your present?" Stan repeated, very brightly, very poised. Mr. Suave in person. "Your present. Oh, your present's in San Francisco. Unpurchased as yet. Rest assured, though, that I have something definite and magnificent in mind. I just haven't been able to order it yet. I'm sorry. I hope you understand."

"Oh," I said, "I understand all right."

I tried to catch his eye and make him feel as rotten as I did, but Stan can be very slippery. He got very busy all of a sudden doing things like changing his clothes and getting out his shaving stuff. He didn't look at me once and we didn't say anything to each other after that. Stan began to whistle a song called "Jim O'Shea." He was still whistling and dialing Luigi's to make a reservation as I walked out the back door.

I didn't wait to tell him where I was going, partly because I was mad and partly because I hardly ever do anyway. It was only six o'clock and this was June. It wouldn't be dark until nine. And Stan knew I could take care of myself in the woods and on the beach. I ought to be able to. I was born here. So I knew he wouldn't worry about me once he came out of his daze of getting ready to see old Troy and noticed I was gone.

If he had worried, I wouldn't have cared.

2
The Cave

We live beside the ocean, practically right in the dunes. The beach is sand. It's a quarter of a mile wide when the tide's out, and you can walk along it for miles without a thing to stop you. You feel free as a gull walking like that, with nothing around you but sand and sky, with the ocean way out there white and steel gray, cold and powerful, all big tides, currents and undertows, crashing its rollers on the beach, able to kill you and pull you miles out to sea if you swim in it and don't understand that it is the Pacific and not an ocean to fool with.

You have to watch the tides anyway, whether you swim or not, because if you don't, even walking on the beach you might end up without a beach to stand on and nothing but a sheer cliff at your back. People have been cut off and trapped like that and drowned. There's quicksand, too, some places, and you have to know where it is or you could be in big trouble.

I know, though. There's not a lot I don't know about the beach here. I've practically lived on it since I was able to walk. I could show you where the deer come down and where the most wild strawberries are on the dunes. I came face-to-face with a bear once in the woods. And I saw a footprint that I think belonged to Bigfoot—what the Indians around here call a Sasquatch. That's a creature that's lived back in the woods for thousands of years. Nobody ever sees them because they're really shy.

But to get back to the night of my birthday: I knew exactly where I was going, even before I left the house. There was this secret cave I knew about where I went sometimes when I really wanted to be alone—where nobody had ever been but me and maybe a few seagulls—and I knew nobody could find me. Which was the best part of it.

I wouldn't have tried to go there that night, though, if it hadn't stopped raining and if there hadn't been three hours of daylight left. It wasn't too far to the cave, but getting inside was tricky. You had to climb the Dogs for one thing. The Dogs was this gigantic rock slide of enormous boulders that was in the water down the beach where it was deserted. It was pretty easy to climb if you didn't look down once you got to the top. Otherwise, all the waves and little whirlpools in the ocean below might make you dizzy or you might begin to think how high up you really were and get afraid to climb back down. Especially if you'd climbed the Dogs before and knew that coming down the other side there was this one place where you had to be careful: a little ledge you had to walk along without much of a handhold and a long fall down if you lost your balance. If you thought about that place too much beforehand, you'd get too scared to try it and would have to go back the way you came. But if you didn't, you were okay. And once past that ledge the rest was easy all the way down.

Once over the Dogs, you weren't on the beach, though; you were on the rocks, the bottom part of the Dogs, with water on three sides of you. That was where the caves were. But unless you were lucky and saw a gull walk into a crack in the rocks, you wouldn't even know there was anything there but rocks and sea and sky.

If you were lucky like I was and followed the gull, you would find yourself inside the Dogs. There were several caves there, all light because the boulders that made their ceilings didn't meet at the top so you could see part of the sky. You wouldn't find my cave, though, because those caves were like labyrinths, and to find mine, you would have had to stumble on it by accident, like I did, and that wouldn't be possible: once I found it, I camouflaged its opening.

It was super wonderful once you got inside: stone walls a hundred feet high and a tiny patch of sky for a ceiling, and for a floor, a white sand beach with mini-rocks and a mini-tide that ebbed and flowed but never covered the beach entirely. And the best thing about it was that it was all mine, a mini-world with only one person in it, namely me—so much my own I sometimes felt like I hadn't found it, I'd invented it.

Because of what happened there on my birthday I remember everything I did that night from the moment

I entered the cave. First, I sat down on the large flat rock that was on my mini-beach. Then I opened a bag of barbecue potato chips that I chanced to bring along and got ready to sit and eat and do some serious thinking.

I had a lot to worry about: Stan and Troy and my life—like why I was so miserable all the time. And I wanted to start in right away because I had to get it all done before night came down. I didn't want to have to climb back over the Dogs in the dark. So that was why I only wasted a minute or two being mad at Stan the Rat for messing up going to Fat George's before I settled down to it. But then, just as I was getting ready to begin worrying—I mean, I started to think about my mom instead. Don't ask me why. I didn't want to think about her at all. But I started to just the same. I couldn't help it.

The waves came in and out, in and out, as the sea came closer and closer to my sneakers. I sat there and watched it come. I thought about my mom and Stan and me and about the accident (for the millionth time) and listened to the waves ask the same question over and over again. Not how it happened, that was easy. The guy in the other car was drunk and on the wrong side of the road going about eighty. He came around a blind curve, and there was a head-on collision. So it was not How? But Why? Because what happened made no sense. Any way you turned it around and thought about it, it ended up as something terrible that happened for no reason. I mean, there was my mom, somebody important and wonderful, here today and gone tomorrow with no warning and for no reason. That was the second worst thing. The first worst thing, the thing I couldn't get used to, was that she was gone forever.

I don't know why I thought of her just then. I mean, there I was with nothing but seaweed to blow my nose on. And anyway, who wants to come back from the beach looking as if they'd been bawling their head off? Is that cool or what? Besides, you always meet somebody, usually the last person you'd want to see you like that, like the girl you don't know who you always pass in the hall between second and third periods. But ready or not, there she was all the same—my mom.

She was wearing this pair of old jeans she really liked, with the place on the back pocket where a peace sign had once been sewn—you could still see the shape of it—and the faded old sweatshirt she always wore to the beach.

She stood in my mind the way she always stood when she was alive: sort of easy and careless, with all her weight on one foot, more like the way a kid stands than a grown-up person. She bit gently on the ball of her thumb, the way she always did when she thought about something, with her head down and a little to one side so that her hair fell in a curve that was like a bird's wing across her cheek and hid part of her face. Her feet were bare. My mom had these really pretty feet, all narrow and high arched with straight, pretty toes. I guess her feet and her smile were the prettiest things about her. Not that what was in-between was bad or anything, either. I just mean the rest of her wasn't what you'd call spectacular. She didn't have the kind of looks that would knock your socks off or anything. That is, until she smiled.

When she smiled—did you ever see the sun come out for just one second on a dark day at the beach and lay sudden brightness on the ocean? That was the kind of smile she had. If you were happy, it came out and sparkled for you in her eyes and was happy, too. But if you were hurt or in trouble, that's when it was really good, because it helped you out and fixed everything: just caught you up and pulled you out of the storm, sat you down by the fire, gave you something good to eat, and made you see, without any words at all, that no matter how bad things looked at the time, everything was really positively okay forever. Because somebody loved you. That was the kind of smile it was.

When I was really little, I thought it was all mine. It was always there for me somewhere in her face, in her eyes, or around her mouth. So I thought it belonged just to me. I lived in that smile when I was little. I used it for everything: to lean against when she told me stories or as my big audience to watch me do awesome stuff like jumping down four steps at a time or standing on one foot. I took it to bed with me to hide in from the dark at night. And when I got too old for all that stuff, I never gave it up. I kept it with me all the time. Only in this private and secret place inside myself where nobody else could see it. So that even though she was gone and could never be with me again, in any solid place, like where I sat on my twelfth birthday, I still had the smile. It was on her face as she stood there in my mind that night. And when I saw it, what happened every time I saw it happened again: a sort of little light came on inside me and whatever was dark in there just disappeared.

You would've liked her all right. Because there were lots of things about her that were very, very cool. Like the games she made up for us to play when I was really little: Prowlers and Clockwork People and Squaresville, all funny or exciting or interesting. Take Clockwork People, for instance. Anybody would've liked to play that. You just—aah, forget it. It hasn't a thing to do with what I'm telling you. Except that it was just one of those cool things about my mom. Like her eyes. They weren't anything special, like being extra large or an unusual color or having long thick lashes or anything. They were just brown eyes. But there was this one really cool thing about them: whenever she laughed, they sparkled. I mean, they really sent out little lights, the way shallow brown river water does when it's in the sun.

And besides all that, there were a couple of things about her that weren't terrifically important or anything, except that if you knew about them they made it hard, if not impossible, to see how she could really be dead, a dead person and everything, somebody who was really gone from you forever. Like, for instance, her baloney sandwiches.

She ate them all the time. She liked to eat them late at night when she was all by herself. And where she liked to eat them was at the kitchen table, so she could look out the window at the black ocean sometimes while she read a murder mystery. She was particular about the sandwich and the murder mystery. The sandwich had to be made with white bread, two slices of baloney, and lots of mayonnaise, with a big dill pickle on the side. The murder mystery had to be English and not gruesome or anything. And she didn't like to be teased about either one or have them mentioned. I used to do it sometimes, though, just to see her get mad. She always did, but not very. She never got very mad at anything Stan or I did or ever stayed mad for long.

Another thing was birds.

If my mom found a baby bird, or anything else that was hurt, the way she picked it up was something else about her that was really cool and made it hard to think of her as somebody who could die and go away forever. I mean, she was so careful when she did it: really, really gentle. She always sort of held her breath, like what she was doing was not only the most important thing in the world, but maybe the only important thing. And she never cared how much time or trouble it took to make it get well again, either.

Come to think of it, maybe that was one of the reasons no one would ever call my mom the world's greatest housekeeper. I mean, she wasn't exactly terrible. She washed the dishes and everything. But we had dust mice and cobwebs in our house, so that she always said how the place was a mess and that we were going to have to get busy and do something about it. Right away. Tomorrow.

Only tomorrow never came because something else always came up: berries to be picked because it was blackberry season or time to make Christmas ornaments (she loved to do that) or something else that was lost or hurt or needed her attention.

Until the accident there was so much good stuff in our lives. But all of it had my mom in it, was my mom. Really. And all of it was just so neat and perfect that Stan and I couldn't even talk about any of it after she was gone or think about it or remember how good it was.

The thing was, we always had so much fun together. It seemed to me like we were all the same age sometimes. What I mean is, we sort of all played together. We had these wild times when we chased through the house and acted as silly as we wanted because there was no one to see us and laughed so hard we nearly wet our pants. It happened all the time but started in all different ways.

My mom might pass Stan reading in his chair and he might reach out and slap her on the behind and say something retarded but usually quite funny. Then my mom would pretend to get mad and grab him. Then they'd wrestle a little or chase through the house with my mom out to get Stan and with me helping sometimes one, sometimes the other, until we all ended up on the floor, rolling around laughing and trying to catch our breath. Then Stan would hold out his hand to pull my mom up and they'd walk away holding hands. They held hands a lot or walked with their arms around each other. They liked to keep in touch.

When I was really little, my mom and I went out on the dunes a lot. If you don't happen to know what a dune is, don't believe it if somebody says they're just hills that go for miles along the ocean, because they're a lot more than that. In fact, if you look at it the right way, the dunes can be almost anything you like: space, privacy, quiet— the place to go for time and a chance to think, the place to be yourself for a change. The dunes are shells and wild grasses, secrets and freedom. Promises made and kept. The place that is away. All according to who you are and how much you see. And you don't even have to have seen one to know what I mean.

Anyway, my mom liked the dunes a lot. And it was good to go there with her because she knew all about them, like what wild animals made the tracks we found and the names of all the birds and plants and insects that lived there. She never hurried me. She always let me look at stuff as long as I wanted, was patient to answer all my questions, and was never cross. The only thing that ever made her mad was if somebody tried to hurt even so much as an ant there on the dunes. Or anywhere.

What we'd do, we'd walk until we found a sheltered spot that was away from the wind and the roar of the ocean. Then we'd settle there for the morning or after-noon or all day. She'd get out her book and read it while we ate our sandwiches. And I'd sit beside her or run down the beach to look for shells or driftwood. I always looked back to make sure she was there. She always was. Even at night all I had to do was wake up in the middle of a bad dream and she was there to tell me not to be afraid and to take me into bed with her and Stan.

When I was really, really little, I thought she smelled like apples and safeness when she put her arms around me. And whenever I smelled her in the middle of the night like that, the Dark came in and washed me away, past memory and time, to closed eyes, the taste of warm milk and her hair held in one of my fists; with nobody in the world but her and me.

She was always just so nice. What I mean is, she never made Stan and me feel stupid or blamed or bad about anything. She just minded her own business. I don't mean she had no opinions about the way you were sup-posed to act or that she never showed me how to take care of myself or do what I was supposed to, or anything, because she did. All I'm saying is, she was one of those people who knew how to leave other people alone. She never messed with our private thoughts or feelings, because all she wanted was to go along and enjoy life. And that was why nobody cared if she didn't get around to doing stuff other people might think ought to be done or that we had a sort of messed up house, like maybe we did, because it was just so nice to see her happy. Just so cool to have her with us, with everything good and not mean, the way things are supposed to be.

Everybody told us after the accident that she must've died instantly, that she probably never knew what hit her—like she was roadkill or something. As if they thought hearing something as brilliant and comforting as that would make Stan and me feel better. Though even if they'd said something intelligent and nice and not stupid at all, it wouldn't have helped. Nothing would have made us feel better. We were like people who'd been killed ourselves but who still somehow walked around.

We didn't talk to each other much because we had to be so careful what we said. The wrong thing, the slightest touch, on the raw skin of our memory could make us scream. We couldn't talk about anything like my mom or the accident or anything else. Not even stuff we needed to, like having some sort of funeral and everything.

If we could've lit up the sky or hung up two moons or set out the stars to spell her name it maybe would've been all right. We might not have minded a funeral like that. But we didn't want the kind most people had. And we knew my mom hated all funerals. So in the end, since Stan and I couldn't get it together enough to talk about one, my mom's parents, Grandma and Grandpa Snow, had to come all the way from their apple farm east of the mountains to arrange one. And when they got through with it, it was about what you'd expect it to be: it was a funeral all right.

My mom would've hated it. There was a funeral home and a casket and a religious smell that was part dust from the pew cushions and part Easter lilies. There were all the people, who sat in rows, all dressed up for her funeral. They stared straight ahead and tried to look the way they thought people ought to look at funerals: serious, careful not to show how glad they were to be still alive but not crying about it either. While the organ played sad, spooky music like something you'd hear in a haunted roller rink—music for ghosts to glide around on skates to. And I had to smell the lilies and hear somebody my mom didn't even know get up there by the casket and say in this holy kind of voice a lot of stuff about her that you could've said about anybody.

Stan didn't even come to the funeral. I was glad he wasn't there. I wouldn't have been there either if they hadn't caught me and made me come with them to see it all. And I did see it all. Everything. Down to the man who kept looking at his watch while the holy guy prayed for her. And all of it just so brilliant and clear. I could see every spot on every tie and every freckle: all edged with light and so bright it almost hurt my eyes.

That's how everything looked to me while the funeral went on. Yet at the same time, I wasn't there. I know that's weird. But all the same, I wasn't there. While all the stuff went on, the spooky music and the smell from the lilies and Grampa Olmstead's breath whistling in my ear, I was far away from there, down on the dunes where nobody was but me. And my mom. A big wind made whitecaps on the water. We walked the dunes and ate wild strawberries. She smiled at me. We laughed at the funeral.

Afterward I stood with my grandparents so people could come up and tell us they were sorry and all. I nodded my head when I was supposed to and answered everything, but I was really not there. Grampa Olmstead didn't know this of course. He's Stan's father, a thin, beaky old bird with mean yellow eyes, like a seagull's, and the same sort of fierce, indignant, not-too-bright expression eagles have. And he really wasn't all that bright if you stood back and looked at him. He was always mad at somebody or something. That day he was mad at Stan for not showing up at the funeral. And he didn't trust me all that much either, so he stood behind me in his black suit with his dazzling white hair all nicely brushed and kept a bony jittery old man's grasp on my upper arm as if he thought I might break away any second and head for the beach.

Nobody knew where Stan was. I personally thought he was at the beach. I was the only one not mad at him that day because I knew how he felt. I was the only one who felt as bad as he did. I didn't blame him for leaving me alone with the funeral and everything either, because I knew he wouldn't have blamed me if it had been the other way around, and I'd gone away.

Still and all, it wasn't easy. After the funeral there were all these cars with little funeral flags on them and the limo we drove in and the hearse. There was the drive to the cemetery. There was the grave.

And even back home with all the people gone, the day went on forever. I sat in our living room that still had my mom's raincoat hanging on the closet door and listened to the clock tick loud and steady, as if time really passed, and wondered how long this would go on before we woke up from our nightmare and saw she was back in the house where she belonged.

And it was on that afternoon when time stopped and we sat there and listened to silence that I got this idea. I'll tell you what it was. Get ready to scream with laughter. I don't care.

What I thought was: maybe I could get her back. I mean, I knew she was gone and everything and that you were supposed to be gone forever when you were dead. But on the other hand, I knew there was a lot more to my mom than you could put in a casket. So the way I figured it was, she had to be somewhere. I didn't think she'd be someplace like heaven because from what I'd heard of it, I thought she wouldn't like it there. The underworld made more sense, though maybe not the Greek under-world or anything, but the place where the part of a person that never dies could go. It wouldn't be a bad place, I thought. It might even be a wonderful, terrific place. But no matter how good it was, I knew my mom would rather be with Stan and me. And the thing was, I thought that maybe she couldn't get out by herself. That maybe she was like that wife of Orpheus—somebody had to go get her. Like me.

Go ahead. Laugh. But that afternoon, the more I thought about it, the more I believed it, the more it filled my mind. I couldn't get rid of it. I couldn't quit thinking about it either. I knew it was an impossible thing. I couldn't tell anybody about it, not even my friend

Le Moin, because I knew it was too weird. And that as ideas went, this one hadn't much going for it in the way of being possible or anything. The only big thing it had in its favor was it was my only hope.

But I kept on thinking about it long after the day the funeral was over. And though nothing was really the same at all, a lot of it seemed to be the same. What I mean is, I went back to school and kept on eating (sort of) and stuff like that. But the idea of my mom being someplace where I could go and find her stayed in my mind. I thought about it all the time.

I never asked Stan where he'd gone the day of the funeral. We never talked to each other at all, except to say stuff like "pass the salt" if we happened to be eating at the same time. Which wasn't often. And we didn't go away anyplace afterward either, because it wouldn't have helped. You can't get rid of somebody like my mom that easy. She would've come right along with us. So we just hung out where we were. But not together. The good times were over and we knew it. Because my mom was gone. That was all there was to say about it. I went back to school because I had to, and Stan went back to work because he had to. But he stopped writing his book and started on this trip around the world in his bedroom whenever he was home. Neither of us slept a lot but we never seemed to be awake at the same time either, so we sort of stopped having regular meals. We just kept food in the refrigerator and ate whenever we were hungry.

One more thing. I can't remember the first time I ever

heard Stan laugh, but he used to laugh a lot. He threw his head back and did it with his eyes closed. Or sometimes it was just a quiet, pleased little laugh at some private joke of his. He had a lot of private jokes he thought were really funny. My mom and I thought they weren't too bad usually, but sometimes the ones he thought were the funniest—the real knee-slappers—we didn't get at all. It never mattered. Stan always thought they were as funny as ever, even when we didn't laugh. And it was just so nice to see him laugh like that.

I never heard him cry though, not once in my whole life, until after the accident. Then I heard him sometimes in his room. Sometimes I cried myself but it was worse when he did it because I never expected to hear it and it sounded so sad.

I never let on I heard. It was just another one of the things we didn't talk about. Neither of us could stop thinking about my mom or get used to the idea that she was gone forever and wouldn't be back.

That was what hung over our house like a thick brown fog that never went away. It drifted in thicker and thicker until it hid us from each other and we wandered around alone in it and got too far away to talk together or see each other or even hear ourselves call anymore.

I don't know how Stan felt about it. I didn't ask. But I sure knew how I felt. I felt like I was about four years old and lost in some dark place where nobody would ever find me and where I couldn't find anybody either—not Stan or my mom or even myself. And the worst thing about it was *nobody was even looking for me*. My mom was gone, so she couldn't. Stan didn't care. All he wanted was to be left alone. And I couldn't seem to help myself. So for quite a while after the funeral I just lived by myself in this weird brown fog in our weird and empty house. With all our wild and funny times all over, and no one to come and get me out.

Most of the kids I knew kept away from me. I think they were kind of embarrassed at what happened. I know I would've been—like it was a sort of exciting thing to happen: this kid you knew mom's being killed. Somebody you actually knew and everything. But embarrassing too. Because what can you say to somebody like that? So they left me alone. And I was glad they did. I didn't want to be around anybody right then anyway, not even Harold Le Moin, my best friend. Harold was okay. I guess he felt sorry for me and everything, but he didn't know what to say or how to act about it either.

I sat in classes where I was supposed to be. I took the tests I had to and failed. I never did the homework because I couldn't get it together. I thought about other stuff: like where my mom could be and how I might find her and get to her wherever she was, but not about schoolwork. I either forgot to do it or never even heard the assignments. It didn't matter. In my mind I was out on the beach most of the time anyway.

Some of the teachers called me in after school and tried to find out what was wrong and everything. They were okay, but we never really got in touch because

I wasn't there. So they talked, but nothing changed. I just kept on going to school every day and Stan kept on walking around the world in his room.

Then one day Le Moin asked me to walk down to the newsstand and to see if the new issue of *Twisted Tales* was out (*Twisted Tales* was our favorite comic book), and then walk home up the beach. And I said okay. Later on, Stan finished his trip around the world and started to type in his room again. And so, slowly, stuff like that crept in. Le Moin slept over at my house one weekend. Stan and I went to Fat George's for dinner one night. Grampa Olmstead came for an unexpected visit for a week that seemed to last a month. Stan called up a girl with piano legs named Sybil, somebody he'd gone to school with. He took her out to dinner a few times and probably talked her ear off about my mom. I went camping with Le Moin and his family one weekend. We hiked up this mountain and slept in tents and everything. But it wasn't much fun, because Le Moin's mom fussed a lot and really knew how to ruin something like camping. But the thing was I went. And then a little later, Stan forgot Sybil and started calling up girls who looked really good in tight jeans, that you didn't have to talk to much. I guess he realized it didn't help to talk about my mom to anybody. That was the second stage of his weirdness at the time.

The third stage was old Troy. I didn't worry too much about her at first. I just worried about Stan's all around weirdness. I was afraid he might marry somebody out of sheer weirdness and that person would happen to hate me or something. Then later, I started to worry a lot that maybe old Troy was that person. In which case, if that happened, I planned to run away.

The thing is, they never stay, the people who are gone. They come into your mind and then just when you really start to get into having them there—they go away again. And when they do, it feels lonelier and worse than ever.

3
Excalibur

I sat on my white mini-beach the night of my birthday and there she was, plain as anything, with all the stuff she brought with her: the way she loved animals and the dunes, baloney sandwiches and all our good times, and just herself. There she was. And then she was gone. With nothing left but the big rocks behind me, the wash of the water as it nibbled the shore with tiny bites, over and over again, and the clammy feel of cold sand on the seat of my jeans. Maybe it happened because it was the night of my birthday. Or maybe it was because all these things had been building up inside me for a long time. Whatever it was, all I know is that suddenly I felt worse than I'd ever felt in my whole life. It was awful. I wanted to die. I thought how everything in my life was too hard for me to handle. That my problems had no answers. And I didn't know what to do. Then I thought everybody else was the same way I was, that nobody knew what to do about anything. That the older you got the more problems you had, without getting any answers—until one day you found out there *never had been* any answers to anything in the first place. Only problems.

I had a few other thoughts, too. Like how maybe love was like Santa Claus, something people wanted kids to believe in but that wasn't real; that nobody ever really loved or even liked anybody else once they were grown-up—they just pretended to for what they could get out of it, that everybody lied to everybody else about everything all the time and anyway, there was going to be a nuclear war and everybody would be destroyed, so it didn't really matter.

The trouble was it did matter. It mattered so much to me, in fact, that while I was thinking, all kinds of strange things started to happen. I broke into a cold sweat. I got so dizzy I had to put my head down on my arms. It was awful, feeling so scared and alone: like dying. I reached out with my mind as hard as I could for something to hold onto. And there was nothing. Inside my head I heard myself call out, "Is anybody there? If there is, help me, help me."

If I hadn't promised myself to give up exaggerating stuff, I'd say that about then a shaft of light shot down from the sky and illuminated my mini-beach or a great white bird flew over—something dramatic, anyway. It wouldn't be true though. Something powerful happened all right but it was more inside myself, more a thing you felt than something you could see.

I felt better. My dying feeling was gone. Then, once I was all right, I began to notice things again. One of the things I noticed was the silence. It wasn't an ordinary silence, without sounds. I could hear the waves and the cries of the gulls in it. But it was a different kind of silence from any I'd ever felt before. It sort of came up all around me, peaceful and comforting, all calm, like something I knew a long time ago and had forgotten. Only then, when I felt it again, I remembered it perfectly and wondered how I could ever have forgotten it or lived without it.

I don't know how long I sat there but when I got up my worries seemed small and faraway. And the first thing I noticed was something I hadn't seen before. It was in semidarkness at the back of the cave, a big thing in the shadows there. I went closer. Then I walked right up to it and saw it was made of driftwood, gulls' feathers, and shells, with a lining of seaweed—everything you find on the beach—tossed together to make a large, untidy nest.

It hadn't been there before. The cave had always been empty. The sand around the nest was all torn up and pushed into heaps and furrows as if something large had had to leave it in a hurry. I went right up to it and looked inside.

There was a large egg, about the size of an ostrich egg, lying in the nest. It was round, like a turtle egg—all green and blue and gray—soft colors that seemed to melt together yet stay distinct at the same time. There was life in the egg. The colors pulsed with light. Then, as I looked (and almost forgot to breathe), it moved. A crack appeared down one side. The egg rocked gently back and forth. It was opening.

The large crack broke up into a whole root system of

hairline cracks that traveled all over the surface of the shell. A large piece of shell fell into the nest and something moved inside the egg.

The first part of him I ever saw was his little right front arm. It was scaled. The scales were a faint green, as tiny and delicate as goldfish scales or babies' fingernails. They ended in a bronze-colored three-toed claw, like a bird's except that where each toe should be there was a fierce little barbed claw instead. I took a step backward just to be on the safe side.

After the arm broke through, I saw his head. The instant I saw it I realized he was unique, like nothing that had ever been on earth, and that I was probably the only human being who had ever seen anything like him. There will never be another moment like that one.

I wish I could tell you what he was like when I first saw him. I mean, so that as you read this, you could see him too, the way I did. It's very frustrating, because in the first place, I want you to understand how beautiful he was when he first hatched. Just so perfect and so complete. If you could have seen his little head, the way I did, breaking out of the shell—all brave and fierce and perfect, with his eyes a-flickering, living red, like flames that looked straight at you, all proud and fearless, like a hawk's.

You could see right away he was designed for battle. The big toes on each of his feet were pincers with serrated edges. There was a long graceful red ornament at the end of his tail, which looked like it was half sting, half barb. He had moth-soft, soot-colored rudimentary wings growing from his shoulders, but he wasn't a bird or a reptile or a mammal or a star or a flower or a flame, but scaled like a snake, beautiful as a star, fierce as an eagle, bright as a flame: an intelligent creature.

He was a thousand things, Beauty and the Beast become one, his face the face of a beautiful brute: unburnished gold and, like his eyes, always flickering beneath the surface, always changing until—depending how you looked at him—he was either hideously beautiful or beautifully hideous.

That was later though. Right then he was like all newborn things. Once he'd pushed out of his shell he tried to stand up and immediately fell over. He kept on trying while I stood there watching. I was three feet from the nest by that time and completely unable to move. I could hardly even breathe. I didn't know what to do. I didn't want to touch him. Baby or not, he was like a lion cub. He looked dangerous. Accidentally or not, those claws could have ripped me to shreds. Besides, I thought, if he had a mother and she came back (though how she could get into the cave was beyond me, even though obviously she'd got into it before to lay the egg—or had she?). Anyhow, if the baby smelled of humans, I thought she might reject him like some earth birds and animals do. (You see, I was worrying about him already.)

After three more tries he was able to stand upright on his feet, though, and after a dozen more he was out of the nest. That was when he first sighted me with his fierce, flaming eyes. He headed right for me. I didn't move. I was so fascinated I didn't think to move—so fascinated I forgot to be afraid.

Once he was out of the nest, I found I wasn't able to think what he was like at all, only what he wasn't like. He was not like a cub or a fawn or a baby. Not like a unicorn or a dragon. He was about the size of a half-grown collie but looked like nothing but himself: monster shaped, a beautiful monster. I was so enchanted I wouldn't have gone away and left him for anything.

He came right up to me. I took a chance of being shredded by his claws and stayed where I was. He didn't try to hurt me, though. He wasn't afraid and neither was I. We stood looking at each other. I wondered what he thought. If he thought. I sat down on the white sand beach. He came near to where I was. He picked up sand and shells with his terrible claws, looked at them, and threw them back when he had finished. I sat and he walked and for a while I had plenty of questions on my mind.

Where had he come from? Had aliens beamed him down into the nest? And if so, why? Or had some accident, some crisis like a galactic storm forced his mother off course and made her land on earth? Did he even have a mother? But of course there were no answers and after a while I stopped trying to explain him to myself. Who can explain something like that? Nobody. Not even Jacques Cousteau or Einstein could have explained something like him: what he was or where he came from, how he got into the cave, or what he was doing on earth at all. And anyway, while the answers to those questions might be interesting, what mattered was, he was there. And just hatched. And that I felt responsible for him.

I had worries right away about that. Like, what was I supposed to feed him? All living things had to eat, at least all the living things I'd ever heard of. I didn't know about baby monsters—I thought they probably had their own rules. But I thought this one seemed hungry. He seemed to be waiting for something. He sat on the sand on his hind legs like a griffin and watched me with his fiery eyes.

Milk seemed like the most suitable thing (unless he drank blood—he looked like he might). All I had was a Mars™ bar I'd saved from lunch. I wasn't at all sure it was the right thing to give him, but I took it out of my pocket anyway and took a bite, to show him what to do. I thought if he didn't want it, I'd eat it myself.

He wanted it though. He opened his mouth. I saw three sets of pointed teeth, real bone snappers, close on the Mars™ bar, wrapper and all. It was pretty fascinating. Once he knew what his mouth was for, he began to eat other things. I watched him eat a whole pile of seaweed, some sand, a few rocks, which he crunched up as easily as you would a handful of M&M's™. For dessert, he ate my sweatshirt that I had carelessly left lying on the sand.

He seemed to have a pretty good appetite, but he ate very delicately, more like a cat than a dog. And when he'd had enough he cleaned his face and front paws. His tongue was royal blue and as elaborately shaped as a medieval banner, forked at the end and edged along the sides with points, like the leaves of a thistle. After he cleaned his claws he started on his scales. I could have watched him do that forever, his tongue was so precise and delicate and clever, but the sun was setting. The piece of sky I could see was turning a darker blue and I needed light to go back over the rocks. I should've gone right away, but I didn't because it was so hard for me to go.

I hated to leave him there, if you want to know. What I really would've liked to do, what I wanted to do, was wrap him up in my sweatshirt and take him home with me. By that time, you see, I was beginning to talk myself into thinking he was mine. After all, I'd found him on my birthday, so he was like a birthday present. The best birthday present anybody could ever have. But even while I was wishing I could take him with me and trying to talk myself into doing it, I knew it wouldn't work. I could see it all: me trying to keep him a secret, then somebody finding out about him and everybody wanting to see him. After that, it would be out of my hands, your standard horror film: the media taking pictures of him and scientists coming to take him away so they could do things to him and find out how he acted when they made him sick or mad or crazy. Besides all that, it would be a terrible thing to do. He was a baby now but he would grow up and then he could never be anybody's pet, anymore than a star or a flame could be. And anyway, even if I had been able to get myself past all these objections, I couldn't have wrapped him in my sweatshirt because he'd eaten it.

In the back of my mind I was afraid his mother might come during the night and take him back to wherever they'd come from and I'd never see him again. In a way, I sort of hoped she would. He was so little and perfect, and that way he'd be safe. In another way, though, I didn't want her to come, because at least for a while I felt he was mine.

I was thinking all this stuff while I was getting ready to leave, piling up more sand in the nest and sort of fixing it up. When I was finished, I went over to him and touched him with one finger—just in case I was dreaming or something and he wouldn't be there the next day. I wanted to see what he felt like.

His scales were soft and flexible and bent at the edges under my fingers. He stood still and let me touch him as if he liked what I was doing. He even moved closer to me, which made me remember how young he really was; and for just that one instant, while I stroked his scales, he was really mine, the way any baby animal would be. But the next instant he moved away from me and was not like a baby animal or anything else I'd ever seen, but something poised, strange, and powerful already. I realized all over again how wonderful he really was, as he stood an arm's length away, balanced so delicately on his terrible claws, and looked at me out of his fiery eyes. And it was this realization that made me want to name him and told me what to name him—maybe it was dumb to think it, but I didn't want to leave him alone there in the cave all night without a name. What I mean is, a name seemed like a way of protecting him somehow, of fixing his identity in the cosmos, so it could be remembered where he was and that he still needed to be taken care of.

I named him "Excalibur," after King Arthur's sword. And before you think that's dumb, too, let me explain. We'd been reading about King Arthur all semester in Lit I and you know the part where the arm clothed in white samite appears out of the middle of the lake, holding up the great war sword Excalibur in its hand? Well, I liked that part because I kept thinking how lethal and powerful it must've looked blazing away in the sunlight before they stuck it in the stone. And how it was something magical, something nobody could explain or explain away: like the egg I found in the cave. So— because my creature was dangerous and shining and magical, too, and the only thing I'd ever seen terrific enough to be called Excalibur—that's what I called him.

4
The Great Salmon Caper

On a scale of one to ten of places I hated to be, school was number two, right up there after the medieval torture chamber. Being there the day after I found Excalibur wasn't too bad, though. I thought about him practically every minute: how he looked, how I was going to see him as soon as school was over, and whether he'd changed any since yesterday. This got me painlessly through most of my classes.

The typewriter was rattling away in Stan's room when I got home so I didn't disturb him. I just walked quietly around the house collecting all the stuff I needed before I left. I'd worked it all out earlier that afternoon in U.S. history class while the rest of the class doodled and passed notes and slept through the Monroe Doctrine.

I planned a sort of experiment. What I thought was, Excalibur had eaten all that stuff the night before, like shells and seaweed, but I didn't really know if that was the stuff he liked or needed. Or even if it was good for him. So I got together all the food I could find in the refrigerator that afternoon, put it in a duffel bag, and took it to the cave to try it out on him, to sort of let him decide what he needed to eat. I still have the list of stuff I took that day:

one can opener
one bottle opener
strawberry Pop Tarts™
canned artichokes
a pint of milk
barbecue potato chips (in case I got hungry myself)
canned spinach
a bottle of Pepsi™ (in case I got thirsty)
hot dogs
one whole salmon
one blanket for the nest

The salmon was a stranger to me. I found it lying on a platter on the top shelf of the refrigerator. I never saw it before; it hadn't been there that morning. I don't know why I took it. I knew better. Unless it was because Stan and I hate salmon anyway. But I knew it was probably there for dinner and that Troy was probably going to come over and cook it.

It turned out I was right about Troy.

Just as I was going out the door, Stan, who can hear around the loudest typewriter, called from his room, "Brady?"

"What?"

"Where are you off to?"

"Beach," I said.

"Okay, but be back by seven. Troy's cooking. And watch your step. There's some tricky places down there."

"I know," I said. "Okay."

If you think it was easy to get myself and the duffel bag to the cave, you're dead wrong. It was awful. With all the stuff inside it that duffel bag weighed a ton. I had to drag it down the beach and then hoist it onto the Dogs. And that was when my troubles only started. It was like taking some big, dumb, half-wit along, somebody who couldn't think for himself, and it was up to me to get someplace. What I mean is, the duffel bag fell against me at all the wrong times. I nearly killed myself climbing the rocks before I reached the cave. Once I was there it was worth it, though, because when I had part dragged, part fallen over the duffel bag, until I got it to my private beach, I saw Excalibur was still there. I didn't get a good look at him right away because I was too hot and out of breath to notice much at first. Then, I'd lost a sneaker pulling the bag through the crack in the rock and had to go outside to get it before the tide did. But after I picked it up, I went back inside and that was when I really saw him.

He almost took my breath away. He'd grown overnight. He was about the size of a pony and he didn't fit the nest anymore. But that wasn't what startled me. What made me catch my breath was how much more beautiful he'd grown overnight.

He looked a lot stronger. More defined. All the soft little green scales had hardened until they looked like sheets of armor. And they had brightened. They'd turned that shining green-gold color you see on hummingbirds or scarab beetles: all changeable. So that when the light hit him one way he blazed gold and when it hit him another, all emerald green. And the bronze on his neck and claws looked more polished with the claws longer and sharper.

I won't describe his face, because I can't. Except to say that it was smoky gold and mysterious, brute beautiful, and—like thought—always shifting, so that you could never really say you saw it. Yet at the same time, you could look at it forever, and though you might get lost in it, you could never grow tired of it. I don't know . . . it wasn't quite like that either . . . nobody can really tell anybody else about something like Excalibur. Though you might hear it in music sometimes. Some music. If you like music.

Anyway, he looked at me with his beautiful, flaming eyes when I came into the cave and I knew he recognized me and was glad I'd come back. He watched me open the duffel bag and take out all the things I'd brought. I couldn't decide what to offer him first, so I just laid it all out on the beach at his feet and let him choose.

He didn't touch anything at all until I ate a Pop Tart™. Then he ate one. He ate all the Pop Tarts™ then, and when he'd swallowed those, worked his way through the rest of the stuff. I hadn't needed to bring the can opener or the bottle opener. Besides, he ate them after the Pop Tarts™.

He ate the spinach and the artichoke hearts, can and all, in one gulp, like a boa constrictor swallowing a rabbit. When he'd eaten the milk, carton and all, the hot dogs, and the salmon, he started on the blanket, but I stopped him. I didn't know too much about him at the time. I thought he might need the blanket to keep himself warm at night.

The last thing to disappear down his throat was the duffel bag, which I'd forgotten to watch, followed by a handful of small rocks crunched into powder by his triple row of teeth. It had taken him less than ten minutes to eat it all. And I can't say I learned much about his taste in food from watching him do it, either.

The thing was, he ate everything but he didn't act famished. There was nothing wolfish about the way he ate. And he showed no preference either. The salmon, the duffel bag, the sand, all seemed to be the same to him. So there was still no way of knowing if he liked one thing better than the other. I didn't even know if he'd been hungry or not. Watching him made me feel sort of hungry, though, so I sat down on my large flat rock and broke out my barbecue potato chips. I hoped I wouldn't get too thirsty. Excalibur had also eaten my bottle of Pepsi™.

He came over and sat beside me on the sand. He seemed to be glad to be sitting there with me. I ate a chip and then, flicking out his royal blue tongue, he ate a chip. We took turns like that until the bag was empty and he ate that too. Then we just sat together for a while, looking way up to the top of the cave. We sat watching the clouds move across the piece of sky we could see up there, almost drawing our breath at the same time (I thought) as we watched. I knew he was feeling like I was feeling, just easy and calm and happy, sitting there quietly like that.

I don't know the exact moment we started to communicate with each other. All I know is that as we sat there together, it just happened. I had a thought and he answered it. But not in words; the answer came in the shape of a thought in my mind, only I knew it wasn't my thought. It was his. I was wondering for about the millionth time how he came to be there in the first place and if he liked the cave, when suddenly I knew that yes, he did like it in the cave and that he didn't know himself how he got there.

The answer came so clear in my mind that I knew it was Excalibur speaking to me in his own way. I got very excited, of course. *Thrilled* might be a better word or maybe even awestruck would be closer to the way I felt. I probably should have been feeling slightly embarrassed, too, at having been so sure I was the most—and only— intelligent member of our little club in the cave and at not having considered he might be as intelligent as I was— but I was too amazed to even think of that.

Once I got used to the idea of exchanging thought with Excalibur, though, a million things thrashed and flopped around in my head like fish in the hold of a fishing boat. When I was finally able to sort them out and turn them into questions, our silent conversation went something like this:

If he didn't know how he got there, did he know where he came from?

He came from where everything comes from.

I didn't know what he meant. Where was that?

He couldn't tell me. You either knew or you didn't. If you didn't, you had to find out for yourself.

I still didn't know what he meant, but I thought, Forget it. Why hadn't he communicated with me sooner, though, like yesterday?

Yesterday he had still been in the egg. You had to be something that had hatched yourself to realize what a struggle it was to break out of an egg. It took all the strength you had. Then, yesterday he'd had all the other things to do: learn to walk, see where he was, and get accustomed to his environment. He still couldn't fly.

Would he be able to fly eventually?

He thought so. When his wings had grown.

That was one of the things I'd been wondering about, that worried me about him. How much would he grow?

Now that he was hatched, he would never stop growing.

But he would have to stop growing. Everything stops growing when it's mature. Anyway, if he didn't stop growing, he'd get bigger than King Kong, bigger than a California redwood. He'd grow clear up to the sun. There he was thinking like a very recent egg and that showed he didn't know everything.

I was the one who didn't know everything. Growing didn't always mean getting taller or older. And he wasn't stuck in the same shape like I was, either. He could change shape as the need arose and as change was demanded of him. That was real growth.

I looked into his face that was always shifting and

changing under its surface of smoky gold, and I thought: Everything was there. Things that made me feel happier than I'd ever felt before in my life and things that the mere suggestion of froze my spine and turned my eyes to staring ice. What was he? I'd thought all along that he was good, but what was he? Good or evil?

He was whatever I made him.

If that were true, then maybe I was just dreaming him or I was crazy and making him up, so he wasn't real.

He was a lot more "real" than I was!

He spoke in riddles. I couldn't understand most of what he meant, though now I realize he was putting it as simply as he could. So I gave up and decided to be less general and get onto more practical things, like what about food?

What did he need to eat?

He didn't need food because he wasn't made out of the same stuff that I was. He wasn't part of any food chain.

I thought that I wasn't part of any food chain either, but Excalibur only showed his triple row of terrible teeth in a delicate grin when I thought that.

Oh yes, I was. I was quite edible. But he wasn't.

I looked at his teeth, shuddered, and wondered in a small polite way why then had he eaten all that stuff I'd brought with me that day?

Because I wanted him to.

Could he eat anything?

He could eat anything.

Would he eat anything I wanted him to?

Yes, he would eat anything I wanted him to.

For a few seconds after he thought that, I have to admit I got kind of rotten in my mind. I couldn't help it. It was the idea of having all that power. I started to imagine what it would be like if, one of those days, I told him to eat people. I meant terrible people, of course, like murderers, but then before I could stop myself because that's the way things go, I went a little further and had him eating Troy.

I could see it all. Dusk. And there was Troy and Mr. Purcell, who always gave me such a bad time in Woodworking I, out on the lonely dunes. With myself as the evil genius sending Excalibur out with all those teeth and claws to devour them. They would scream and run and try to escape, I thought, but it would be no use—I stopped the whole thing right there though. I sort of liked the idea of myself as the evil genius and of Troy and Mr. Purcell being eaten up, but I felt too cheap, turning Excalibur, who was like a flight of eagles or wild horses running and was all burning gold, into some third-rate killer monster out of "The Late Show."

Out of hundreds of others, there was one question I wanted most to know the answer to, and that was how, when yesterday he hadn't even arrived in the world—he was still in the egg—did he know all the things he'd just told me?

The answer to that was pure Excalibur.

He knew what he told me when he was in the egg. He knew what he told me before he was in the egg.

I guess I never felt so happy in my life. I could've stayed there forever. So I don't know why I suddenly remembered about Stan telling me to be home by seven o'clock, but I did. I looked at my watch. I was late already. It was 7:20.

Excalibur followed me to the cave opening and sniffed at the air coming in from the sea. I knew at that moment he wanted to come with me and a cold little fear woke up inside me for the first time. What if Excalibur decided to go out and see the world whether I wanted him to or not?

I thought that he couldn't come with me. He wasn't strong enough. They would see him if he went out there beyond the cave and onto the rocks and they'd catch him.

Who would?

Anybody. Everybody. The Coast Guard. The people at the marine biology station. And if they caught him, they'd try to find out about him. They might kill him altogether, doing that. He'd better stay in the cave. It was safer.

If that was what I wanted, he would stay.

I thought that I'd be back tomorrow. And so I left him there.

5

The Spanish Inquisition

I knew I was in trouble the minute I walked into my house. It felt different. Too quiet. Nothing was happening, no music playing, no talking. But somebody was home. I could feel people in the living room waiting for me to close the back door and come on in. When I did, I saw I was right. Stan sat in one of our two armchairs. Old Troy sat in the other.

I was wearing sneakers, but I made a deafening racket all the same as I walked across the floor through all the silence. Nobody said "hello." Nobody said anything. I might as well not have been in the room. Stan just sort of stared away out the window with this funny look on his face I'd never seen before. And old Troy stared straight through me like I was transparent or something. It felt like I was being ignored all right. Only Stan never ignored me in my whole life before, so at first I thought I must be wrong.

I thought something very serious must be going on, so I looked around and then—all at once—I realized what it was: there was going to be a trial. I didn't know what about yet. But I could see a court had been already set up. And I knew who the people in it were. Stan and old Troy were the judges. And I was the accused.

Oh, man. That was a weird feeling. It was terrible. I can't even start to tell you how it made me feel; because no matter what I did, there'd never been a court or a trial in our house before.

There had been times when Stan and I had had to talk things over, but we always did it by ourselves, privately. I usually ended up saying I was sorry and I'd never do whatever it was again. Then after that, if anything had to be changed or fixed up or worked out I'd do it, and that would be that. I never felt bad about it afterward or anything. But just standing there that day in front of them like that made me feel bad already; as if I were the sort of person nobody liked, maybe even somebody who ought to be on trial for something, it didn't matter what.

I once saw a film about the Spanish Inquisition. It was pretty gross, all those people who hadn't even done anything were burned at the stake and tortured and everything. They got dragged through the streets in this sort of procession that ended up at the stake and there were all those people with hoods and this slow awful sounding churchy chant going on. I mean, that film was really gross. When it was over, I was sort of sorry I'd watched it. But anyway, before they were burned at the stake all these people had a trial in this palace. The judges were called "Grand Inquisitors" and were pretty terrifying because they wore these long black robes and weird-looking hats and everything. They sat up on high seats above the crowd and were the ones who sent all those people out to be burned alive. The worst thing about the whole film was that it was about stuff that really happened. People really did that once.

Anyway, I thought of those Grand Inquisitors when I saw Stan and Troy as they sat in those big chairs and stared at me.

It was quiet in our living room, but not a nice quiet. It was more like an awful silence. The palms of my hands, which never sweat, sweated. I wondered what I'd done. And knew it was the Spanish Inquisition all right.

"Aren't you a little late?" Stan said finally.

When I said I guessed I was, he asked me what I had to say for myself.

Stan never says stuff like that. And he didn't sound like himself when he said it either but more like an actor with bad lines who didn't quite know how to deliver them to make them come off. I sort of smiled at him when he said it—I couldn't help it—but he pretended not to see me, because he wasn't Stan at the moment. He was the Grand Inquisitor. You could tell. The weird hat was there all right, right in place on the head, even if you couldn't actually see it.

"Well?"

"I forgot what time it was," I said.

Nobody said anything after that. I slid a look at the other Grand Inquisitor. She was right in character all right, thumbscrews and rack within easy reach, all set to call the guard to haul me away to the stake. There was a little straight line between her eyebrows and the rest of her face looked all pale and annoyed. I could see that if it were up to her, I was as good as dead. I still didn't know what I'd done though, except maybe be late.

"Where were you?" Stan asked. And he frowned at me. Stan never frowned like that.

"At the—" I cleared my throat because my voice came out all weird. There was a lot of anger banging around the room but I couldn't tell where it was coming from. It made me feel strange. My hands got all cold. I felt sick to my stomach. I started to seriously wonder what I'd done.

I found out right after that.

"And where are the things you took?" Stan was the one who asked. The other Grand Inquisitor never asked any questions. She just stared at me with the old burning eyes that were just like the Spanish Inquisitors' in the film.

"The things I took?" I repeated weakly. I knew I sounded stupid. But I felt so weird by that time, what with being the accused and everything, it was hard to think. I was sort of in a fog. The really strange thing was how our living room had changed. It had the same furniture and all, but it wasn't the same room. It felt different to me, like it was somebody else's now and I didn't belong there anymore. Part of me wanted to bawl out loud like a baby at the idea while part of me would've died of embarrassment if I had.

"The salmon, the artichokes," Stan said impatiently.

"The artichokes," I repeated after him, as if I'd never heard of an artichoke before. I know how dumb that sounds, but I really had forgotten about taking the artichokes and other strangers from our refrigerator that day. It seemed so long ago.

Grand Inquisitor number two made a disgusted little sound and moved sort of restlessly, like she could hardly stand a minute more of all the talk and wanted to get on with the thumbscrews. She caught Stan's eye and without saying a word passed him some pretty unpleasant message of her own. Whatever it was, it made Stan, who'd started to look more like himself, get all weird again.

"Troy is quiet upset, Brady," he said. "She was going to cook that salmon in a very special way for dinner tonight. She had it all planned. Then, when she got here tonight, it was gone."

Old Troy gave me a gourmet salmon-tablecloth-and-candles-wine-and-witty-conversation-plus-music-all-your-fault-it's-gone-you-little-monster look. But she didn't say anything.

"You not only inconvenienced her, but you ruined all her plans," Stan said.

"Me?" I said.

"Aw, come off it, Brady," Stan said. "Who else? You know what I'm talking about. Come off it. Did you take those things out of the refrigerator or didn't you?"

"I guess I did," I said.

If the look old Troy gave me when I said that had been a pizza and I'd eaten it, I would've died instantly. In fact, that look was so deadly it got right to me and started to pull tears up from somewhere inside me. I tried to think of something funny to keep them from coming into my eyes, where everybody could see them. I thought of Excalibur eating up the duffel bag. It worked so well I laughed instead.

That laugh was a big mistake. It was one Le Moin and I got off TV. We used it so much it was almost automatic, but it was also very annoying. It was loud and brainless and sort of got the people who heard it in the old never endings. Le Moin and I liked it but Troy hated it. She jumped when she heard it, like she'd been stuck with a pin.

"You see?" she said to Stan. "You see?"

"Brady," Stan said, "cut that out. . . . Now, come on, why did you do it? Speak up."

They were serious. I could see the shadow of the executioner cast on the bare stone walls by the flickering torches of all those Hollywood extras. "Prisoner at the bar, speak now or forever hold your peace." I heard the chants of monks and smelled fire.

"Did I what?" It was hard for me to remember what we were talking about what with being loaded down with chains and both of them staring at me like that.

"Take those things?" Stan said.

It had all come back to me by that time though, and I decided after some consideration to tell the truth. I knew they wouldn't believe me anyway, so Excalibur would be safe. And no matter what I answered, true or false, one Grand Inquisitor was anxious to send me to the stake whatever I said. So—since it never hurt to be honest—I said, "I needed them for an experiment."

"What experiment?" Stan asked.

I knew he liked stuff like that so I said, "I wanted to see if he'd eat the salmon and all that stuff."

"Who?" Old Stan forgot to frown when he asked.

"Oh," I said, "something I found on the beach."

I was still in the dock being questioned—I was still the accused—but the way Stan looked at me made me feel on top of things again.

"Something you found on the beach," he repeated, "something what?"

He looked intrigued. You could tell for the moment he'd forgotten he was a Grand Inquisitor and I was the accused.

"I don't know what it was," I said. "It was kind of like a baby dragon—or not a dragon, more like a griffin—only not like that either. I don't know, it was a creature, sort of like a—"

I stopped. I gave him the old big-eyed honest look of the born liar. It was sort of neat to say something so fantastic, so purely unbelievable and have it be the truth. How often do you get to do something like that?

"Like what?" Old Stan completely forgot he was supposed to be mad at me. He leaned forward in his chair and looked entertained. Not like he believed what I said, but like he was interested all the same in what I'd say next.

About then old Troy, who'd never stepped down from the judge's seat for an instant, called the court to order.

"This," she said to Stan, "is absolutely incredible. I

don't believe this." She looked at me. "I don't know what kind of game you're playing, Brady," she said in this cold sweet voice like poisoned ice cream she always used when she was really, truly mad, "and frankly, I don't care, because your little game doesn't particularly interest me. But I would like to know why you really took my salmon and my artichokes that I planned to cook tonight. I really would be interested to know that. I think it might tell us a lot. So I would like to know now and I would like the truth, please. That is, if you know what the truth is."

I felt pretty guilty by that time about having taken all that stuff, and if there'd been a different look on old Troy's face or if she'd said something else, I probably would've apologized. As it was, all I said was, "I already told you."

"Oh yes," she said, "you met a dragon."

She shrugged her shoulders and made a little face that said as a person, I was definitely a disaster area: some kind of weird sicko who there was probably no hope for.

"What did I tell you?" she said to Stan as if I wasn't even there. "Now what do you say? Was I right or wasn't I about everything I said? You can see there's a problem here, can't you? Perhaps a rather serious one."

For somebody who always remembered to say "please" and "thank you" and all the other stuff people call good manners, old Troy was about the rudest person I ever saw. I didn't know what to do, so I just stood there all loaded down with my chains and felt my palms get sweatier than ever.

"You know what you said was a lie, don't you?" she said.

"It was not," I said. I sort of raised my voice because by that time I was mad too. Enough was enough.

"Brady," Stan said. But Troy gave him another look that said, "Let me handle this." Then she looked at me again. When she spoke it was all soothing and nice sounding to hide the meanness of what she had to say.

"Now, Brady," she said, "I want you to listen to me and think this over, because I'm saying it for your own good." She really did say 'for your own good.' Her very words. I tried to catch Stan's eye when she said it, but he wasn't looking in my direction. I started to smile but quit when she went on to say, "Have you ever thought that perhaps one of the reasons you have such a hard time—maybe why no one likes you at school, for instance—is because no one can believe anything you say?"

There was a dead silence after that. Troy smiled at me. I felt like I'd been hit over the head and stunned like a calf about to be turned into a piece of veal. I thought it was mean of her to say what she had in front of Stan. His opinion of me was pretty important and everything. And the funny thing was, before she said it, I hadn't noticed how hungry and tired I was, but right afterward, I felt all empty and so tired I was about ready to drop to the floor.

But just about then Stan, who'd been looking out the window while all this went on, suddenly woke up and came to life and sort of broke the spell he'd been under.

"Hey, hold on there," he said. "Wait a minute."

He sounded like he hadn't made up his mind yet whether to just laugh it off or get mad.

"What are you talking about?" he said to old Troy. "Lots of people like Brady." He looked half-amused and half-annoyed.

"Who likes you at school, Brady?" he said to me.

"Le Moin," I said out of my pale gray fog of tiredness. "Sometimes."

"Who else?"

"That's all," I said. I didn't even smile. What with climbing over the rocks with the duffel bag and missing dinner and being in the Spanish Inquisition, I was so tired that I'd lost interest in what went on. I guess Stan felt the same way, because he suddenly stood up. I could almost see him pull off his Grand Inquisitor hat and step down from the judge's seat.

"Aaah," he said as if he were suddenly bored by the whole thing, "who cares if a lot of stupid people like him or not? Brady's okay. He's cool. Forget the stupid salmon. Let's all eat out. Come on, I'll take you to Luigi's."

But old Troy wasn't about to let it end so easily and just drop being a Grand Inquisitor like that. She looked at Stan and shook her head.

"No-I-don't-think-so," she said, all thoughtful and serious, still the Big Judge. "I don't want to go anywhere with Brady. Not until he apologizes and tells us what really happened to my salmon. I'm sorry, but I don't happen to think someone should be rewarded for telling an outright lie and getting away with it."

"I told you what happened. A creature ate it."

It felt good to tell the truth to somebody like her and not be believed. I felt better anyway after what Stan said. But old Troy didn't. You could tell she was about to lose her temper because she looked so mad. She frowned at Stan and me.

"I don't understand you," she said to Stan. "He ought to be made to tell the truth." She sounded ready to cry.

"I tried," Stan said, but you could tell he'd lost interest in the whole thing and that for him, at least, the trial was over. "What do you want me to do? Shoot his dog?"

"He hasn't got a dog," old Troy said. And when she said it, Stan sort of smiled to himself in a mean way. He has no patience with people who don't catch on to stuff right away. All he said though was, "You want to eat at Luigi's or not?"

"Not with Brady. Unless he tells us what really happened."

"Brady can stay here," Stan said. He grinned at me. "And reflect on the error of his ways."

"And is this all there is going to be to it?" old Troy asked with the glint of the headman's ax still in her eyes.

"What else?" Stan said carelessly. "You want me to hang him up by his thumbs or something?"

"I don't want to go anyway," I said.

"All right then," old Troy said, "I'll go." She still looked pretty mad but you could see she was climbing down some. "But let's go somewhere closer. Luigi's takes too long and I'm hungry."

"Okay," Stan said agreeably. "Where?"

"How about Fat George's?" She didn't look at me or anything when she said it. She was too smart to do that, but it didn't matter.

She'd ruined herself with Stan all the same, if only temporarily. You can fool part of Stan all of the time and all of Stan part of the time, but you can't fool all of Stan all of the time. Old Troy fooled him better more often than anybody else, but that time she blew it. He knew what she was doing for sure. And he gave her this very funny sharp look, like a man who'd just added up some numbers and got an answer he didn't like. But all the same, when Troy picked up her jacket to go he got ready to go, too. Then he looked at his watch, smiled at me, and said, "Eight twenty-five. Are you aware that *The Creature from the Black Lagoon* will be on Channel 22 in five minutes?"

I hadn't been.

"All right," I said. *The Creature from the Black Lagoon* was one of my all time favorites, as Stan knew very well. When they left I was so busy getting Channel 22 I didn't even say good-bye. I just waved a hand in their direction.

For a miracle, there was no ice hockey or anything. *The Creature* really came on at eight-thirty the way it was supposed to. I didn't go hungry either. There was plenty left to eat in the house. During the first commercial, I made myself a baked bean sandwich on white bread with a glass of milk. After that I didn't so much as shift my weight on the floor until the film was over.

It felt good just to sit there and watch something I liked and not be sad or worried for a while. *The Creature* was as great a film as ever. But then, when a foreign film came on after it, I guess I fell asleep, because the next thing I heard were voices in our front entryway. They sounded all intimate and peaceful, like Stan and his ghoul fiend were getting along for a change. They spoke as if they didn't realize I was there on the couch, and in pretty low voices, but I heard everything they said. I heard Troy's voice first.

"But don't you see," she said, "that it would be for his own good? Face it, Stan, Brady has some serious emotional problems. They're solvable, probably, but they won't just go away. You'll have to do something about them."

"I don't know," Stan said. He sounded pretty serious for Stan. "I don't think he'd like it. He might feel he was being sent away. And he's used to lots of freedom. Boarding school—"

"Oh," old Troy said, "I don't think boarding school is the answer either. Not for Brady. What he needs is a good military academy. Someplace like Stoneygate."

"Where?"

"Stoneygate Military Academy. My brother went there. He loved it."

"He would," Stan said.

Old Troy's brother's name was Randall but he liked

to be called Randi. He spelled it that way, too. He had a little red-brown mustache, eyes that were too close together, and a blank expression. Taken all in all, he was the perfect, exact opposite of the way any thinking person would want to be.

"Just what do you mean by that?" old Troy asked. Randi was one of the things they always argued about.

"Oh nothing," Stan said. "Just that I don't think Brady would like a place like that."

"Like?" old Troy said. "The question is hardly whether he'd like it or not. That's not why he'd be going there."

"Well then," Stan said, "why would he be going? If he didn't like it?"

I couldn't see him because I had to keep my eyes closed but I heard the way he sounded, which was amused. I knew he was being annoying on purpose. And you could tell when old Troy answered that she was getting annoyed.

"Because," she said, "someone like Brady needs discipline, for one thing. Badly."

"Brady's all right," Stan said in an offhand way. "He's okay. You just have to understand him."

"But he's not," old Troy said. "Open your eyes, Stan. He's not okay! Look how he was tonight; lying—call it fantasizing if you like—about dragons and all that escapist nonsense. And when we tried to get the truth out of him he was completely unreachable. He just hung onto his fantasy . . . and if you want my professional opinion, I think he's in danger of becoming entirely alienated. He's obviously having trouble distinguishing between what is real and what is not. This is serious."

"I don't see what going to military school would do for him," Stan said, "besides giving him sore feet."

"All right, be funny about it," old Troy said, sort of bitterly, "but let me tell you, Stoneygate would give him what he so desperately needs."

They said all this in furious whispers out there in the hall, but I heard everything. Once in a while I looked at them from under my eyelids. You could tell by the way they looked and sounded that the whole subject had been gone into before, earlier in the evening, and then come up again, unexpectedly, there in the hall, and that they hadn't planned to stop and talk about it there.

"Such as?" Sam asked.

"Involvement," old Troy said. She loved words like that. "Self-discipline, required sports. Some healthy interests for a change. And some boys his own age to knock the nonsense out of him." She said the last thing with a lot of pleasure, I thought.

"And anyway," she said, sort of more gently, "if we go away on a honeymoon in September right after school starts, he'll have to be somewhere. He can't just rattle around alone in the house, can he? It wouldn't be fair to him, would it?"

"I guess not," Stan said. He always hated to argue about stuff and Troy knew it, too. "I'll have to think about it," he said.

"Nothing to think about," old Troy said. "Really." She

sounded pretty definite all right. I knew if something didn't happen to change everything, she'd probably get her own way. She usually did.

They said good-bye. I kept my eyes closed. I heard the back door shut and old Troy's car drive away. Stan came over to the couch. Through my closed eyes I felt him stand beside it and look down at me. Then he put something on the coffee table beside the couch. I smelled cold grease and pickle and knew it must be a Mastodon from Fat George's. The smell made me almost as sick as the idea of being sent away some place where crowds of 'boys my own age' waited in line for the chance to knock some sense into me.

I pretended to be asleep when Stan put a blanket over me before he went upstairs, but I didn't really fall asleep for a long time after that. I just lay there. I thought about Excalibur for a while; I wished I were an alien from outer space, or a tree growing in some trackless wilderness in Canada, or anything but myself, living in that house without my mom, with only Stan; waiting for old Troy to come live there in her place and send me away to military school.

It was about then that I saw the time had come to get out of that mess, put a stop to everything, and get my mom back. I had no idea how to do it. In fact, until I'd found Excalibur, I hadn't really believed it could be done. Or if it could be done, somehow, that I was somebody who could do it. But once I found him I saw that everything was different from the way I'd always thought it was. That reality was something nobody really knew much about at all. Excalibur was proof and promise that there was more to everything than most people could imagine in a million years. He was real in that cave. And if I could find something as wonderful, as unimaginable as he was, then I could find the way to my mom and get her back. Nothing was impossible, after seeing Excalibur. There were no impossible things.

I thought the beach was the answer. It was the biggest, wildest thing I knew and the closest to everything important. It held all the questions and all the answers, all the secret things there were, within itself. I thought I'd go down there in the morning, walk along the waterline, and no matter how long it took, I wouldn't leave it until I'd found out how to find that line between the living and the dead and how to cross it. Because I had to get my mom back. I had to. I couldn't stand it anymore without her.

6

Famous Monsters #4

I saw it the next morning practically the minute I opened my eyes: my present with HAPPY BIRTHDAY scrawled in big letters right across the paper. It was the thing I wanted most—next to the VCR we couldn't afford yet. It was *Famous Monsters #4*, sent by mail from San Francisco.

Unless you collect comic books, *Famous Monsters #4* may not sound like any big deal. But if you do, you know how it feels to get that certain one, that rare, hard to get copy you've wanted for years and never thought you'd own. And you'd see why I could hardly wait to show it to Le Moin right away, too. He collects "Super Heroes" only, but I knew he'd understand how I felt and be almost as excited as I was when he saw it.

It was weird though. On that morning, once the first excitement of having *Famous Monsters #4* at last wore off, gloom settled down all around me. One second the sun was out, everything was nice and light, and then the next second everything was dark again, darker than ever. I can't explain it unless it was because I began to remember other birthdays, like the one when I was six and the one last year when I was eleven—when my mom was still around.

It felt pretty strange, too, to be living in the past, like some old man or something. But that's how it was in those days. Every time something sort of good happened, instead of being happy about it, I always started to remember my mom and how much better things had been when she was around.

Like birthdays: I appreciated all the time and money Stan must've put into getting *Famous Monsters #4*. It was a neat present and just what I wanted and everything. And I realized things couldn't be exactly the way they used to be. But all the same, I couldn't help thinking how all my old birthdays had been, I mean, really something—not just a present somebody put down next to your pillow at night for you to find in the morning—but something that was just all wonderful and neat that happened, something you could remember forever, all the rest of your life.

Like last year when I was eleven.

We went down to the beach at night for my birthday. We built this big bonfire. Then Stan and my mom sat beside it while the rest of us—me and three other kids, Eric, Jon, and Katie, two brothers and a sister who don't live here anymore—went wild on the beach.

We made up this game about this thing from the sea that was half monster and half mummy that hid in the dunes. We took turns being "it" and hiding. It was cold for that time of the year. My mom brought blankets for us to wrap up in, and she and Stan wore sweaters even by the fire. But we weren't cold because the game was all run and chase. We ran up and down the dunes, jumped and fell all over each other and yelled and argued about who got caught and acted too young for our age. And we yelled our heads off that night, half from fear of the thing. You know how it is: after dark if you're playing a game, even if you know who's the thing, part of you is never sure it's really him and not a real thing. And half because we were out so late and it was dark and we were someplace where we could yell as loud as we wanted. I yelled the loudest that night because it was my birthday and I knew we were going to have hot dogs and marshmallows cooked on the fire and everything, and I was just so happy.

Later, after we ate, Stan set off fireworks. Some blue and green rockets and a few Catherine Wheels he'd got a hold of somewhere. They looked all pretty and dangerous in the night sky. My mom was worried because she said Stan hadn't done them right and he was lucky he still had his fingers. And Stan just laughed at her but the rest of us believed her, and the air smelled perilous, like war. Then we set off a string of firecrackers and Stan really did burn his fingers then, so that a patch of skin turned shiny charcoal gray. But he said it didn't hurt too much. Afterward he sang "Jim O'Shea" and recited "The Walrus and the Carpenter" so he couldn't have felt too bad.

My mom sat by the fire and looked out into the darkness, where the sound of the ocean boomed away beyond the dunes. She smiled and listened but didn't say much. All the same, she was as much there as Stan was, with all his fireworks and songs. And more than anything else—the hot dogs and the fire, the running over the dunes, and the big stars that looked all silver and flashy in the night sky—the best part of my birthday was that she was there.

I never forgot that birthday. I guess I never will. That day as I stood in my bedroom before school with *Famous Monsters #4* in my hand and remembered it, I started to think stuff that was pretty weird: like how maybe some days, my eleventh birthday for instance, kept on happening, only someplace else. Somewhere big and lonely like unexplored parts of Alaska or empty places in the Sahara desert that even the Arabs never knew about. Places like that, where nobody could say they'd seen every mile of. I thought that maybe all the good days people ever had might all be there in that secret place just going on forever.

Stan was awake. I heard him get up and go into the bathroom. After the toilet flushed I went and stood outside the bathroom door and called through it that I was going to the beach.

The door opened. Stan stuck his head out. He looked sleepy and the little place on his head where a bald spot was unless he combed his hair right showed. His eyes were sort of bloodshot, too, so I said, "Hey, man, you look like something the cat would refuse to drag in."

He combed his hair with his fingers and sort of peered at me.

"Where do you get your lines?" he said. "The Goodwill?"

"It looks like you and the Salmon Lady had a big time last night at Fat George's," I said.

"If you mean Dr. Strawbridge," Stan said, "say so."

"I did," I said. "The Salmon Lady. The Fish Person."

"You're a fresh kid. You know that?"

"No offense," I said. "I just meant the person who cooks fish."

"When no one steals it out of the kitchen," Stan said. He gave the bathroom door a longing look as if he would've liked to shut it in my face. Then he looked back at me.

"Did you want anything in particular?"

"Nope," I said. "I'm on my way to the beach for the day."

Just as I said it I thought for one second how surprised he might be later in the day when—if—I came back with my mom. But I didn't think it long. Something about Stan being there so solid and sleepy made me not want to think it when he was around for fear it would be spoiled.

"What about school?"

"I'm giving it up," I said, "for Lent." Then I laughed my brainless laugh, the one I got from TV.

"Come on," Stan said without a smile where there'd always been one before. "School. What about it?"

"There isn't any," I said. "There's a teachers' meeting or something."

I stopped fooling around. I didn't feel like being annoying anymore. It wasn't like Stan to question me or make a fuss like that if I missed one day. It made me feel weird. I sensed a foreign influence there. I wondered if it were old Troy's. I thought it was. It worried me, too. I thought how already the cold winds of change were blowing on Stan and me.

"You need a haircut," Stan said, sort of suddenly and critically, like he'd just noticed it. "You look shaggy."

"You should only have my hair," I said. "Want me to save it when I get it cut? You could maybe paste it over your bald spot."

Stan actually smiled for the first time that day when I said that.

"Oh, and by the way," I said, "thanks for the present. It was magnificently cool."

"My pleasure," Stan said. We bowed to each other ever so politely and for one second it was like old times.

"Well, see ya," I said.

"Turn the burner on under the coffee as you go out," Stan said.

The bathroom door closed again. I knew he was probably starting to shave. And just for one instant before I left, I stood there and closed my eyes and wondered how he would look and what he would say if by any chance at all I was able to do it that day—come home with my mom, safe and sound and back with us forever.

7
The Devil's Finger

The tide was out when I got to the beach that morning and the sand was a long stretch of gray satin. The sky was gray, too, with patches of cold blue in it: a kind of neat thing was that the blue of the sky was reflected in the film of water on the sand.

I thought I'd probably fall and break my neck when I climbed the Dogs that day. I felt so unlucky. But maybe that was the only way somebody like me could reach the land of the dead anyway—only then it wouldn't count because then I'd be stuck in there anyway and could never come back.

The real reason I was depressed, though, was because I was on my way to the Devil's Finger. I really dreaded it. Nobody ever goes to the Devil's Finger. Nobody ever wants to. And I didn't want to either. In fact, I would've given anything not to go there. But the thing was, almost the instant I hit the dunes that morning, I realized that if there was a place where you could be in touch with the invisible, with impossible things like that line between life and death, it would be on the Devil's Finger. Or the beach behind it. And once I thought that, I had to go.

It's such an awful place. Nothing grows there. Not even sea grass because at high tide it's under water. And nothing comes there. Not even birds. Don't ask me why. All I know is, the only things that move on the Devil's Finger are the waves. And they pound the beach like they hate it. The only sounds out there are the hiss and roar, the angry sobs and muttered threats of the voices in the water.

The reason it's called a *finger* is because it goes out farther into the ocean than anywhere else on the coast— way, way out to where there's nothing but water and sky and brilliant white light. Beyond that—nothing. Just the horizon.

But the reason it's called the *Devil's Finger* is because, for one thing, it's a killer beach. When the tide comes in it makes a channel that cuts the Devil's Finger off from the mainland. The channel isn't deep, but the thing is, there's quicksand in it. If you don't know the path through it or don't even know it's there, when the tide comes in you're as good as dead.

And then, for another thing, it's a graveyard: the beach where the ocean lays its dead. Something about the way the current flows makes all the bodies that come out of the ocean wash ashore there: people who die by accident, washed off boats or drowned in an undertow, and the people who die on purpose.

Once they found a dead girl with a rag knotted tight around her throat and nothing else on her but one red sock. Once they found a newborn baby on the sand there. And a week after a ferryboat sank, down near Bear

Harbor, the whole beach was covered with bodies.

Besides dead people, there are always other dead things there like cats, dogs, rats, and birds. Once they found a lamb and once, they say, a dead monkey. I'm glad I never saw the monkey. Or the girl with one red sock . . .

As I walked down the beach that morning, though, I wasn't thinking about any of those things, because what I had in my head was this wonderful, stupid picture of what was going to happen after I found that line and stepped across it: how I'd be instantly in the place where all the people who'd ever died were. I kept on seeing it as this huge enormous place that was something like a waiting room in a railroad station, where all the dead people sat on benches and sort of waited for somebody to come get them. (I know that sounds pretty dumb.) And how when I came in, everybody would sort of look up to see who I was—Thomas Jefferson and Attila the Hun and Elvis and everybody—all hopeful and everything. And how she would look up, too. And then how I'd walk up to her and sort of take her by the hand and she'd smile at me and I'd say, "Come on," or something like that. And how we'd just walk away from that place together and just step over the line that separates here from there. (I *said* it was dumb.)

In fact, part of the time I had trouble with the whole idea of that line. It was like I had two selves. One was all loud and enthusiastic about it, ready to go, deaf, dumb, and blind to reason. Danger? Let there be! This self fairly shouted that nothing could stop it. It would do what it set out to do that day, regardless. It knew what it wanted and brought its own brass band along to drown out all arguments against it.

My second self was totally different. It was slow, stubborn, and almost impossible to convince. It never got excited, but it never quit arguing with my first self either. This self said there was no line and no land of the dead. And anyone who thought there was was retarded. That it was really retarded to go to the Devil's Finger and try to do what I planned (by that time I had this sort of plan in my head). Because what I planned to do was the most dangerous, stupid, childish thing anybody could imagine. And nothing would come of it, nothing at all, except maybe instant death. And so we argued as I walked on.

By that time the part of me that was just moving along had climbed over the boulders that bounded the north side of the beach that lies behind the Devil's Finger, which is called Devil's Bay. It was just as I landed on the sand that I saw them: the three weird sisters. Somebody had lined them up against the rocks like a welcoming committee, so they'd be the first things you'd see. After the first shock of seeing anything at all, they weren't so bad, though. Worse things had been seen on that beach.

The instant I saw them I knew what they were supposed to be because when I was younger I'd made them myself. What you did was take the sea kelp that washed up on the beach, the kind with the dark green bulb on one end that's shaped like a head with long strands of seaweed that's rooted like hair on it, and scratched a face on it with a sharp rock or something. Then you had a mermaid. It was always pretty neat how real she looked the minute you did it.

I didn't know if it were accidental or not, but the ones propped against the rocks looked threatening: sort of wild and demented at the same time, with their scratched-on, staring eyes like insane guardians of the beach, with just enough aliveness to make me have to look over my shoulder once I was past, to be sure they hadn't moved or anything.

I wondered who'd put them there.

The beach ahead looked as lonely as ever: just a long stretch of sand with gloomy looking black boulders scattered over it. And midway to the Devil's Finger, this tall stone column they call the Needle. It was weird to see no flash of birds' wings in the air or hear the screams of gulls and to think that the only birds that ever came to that beach were dead ones.

I looked down at the other end of the beach and saw the black hole in the bluff that I always called the Grotto. I called it that because to me, *grotto* was always a sort of scary word for a scary place, and this hole in the bluff was a weird place to go to. It's dark in there and full of restless, muttering waves that hit its sides and then echo back with this distant boom that's all sad and sort of ominous. Like the sound of cannon-fire from some ancient, bloody battleground.

Another thing about it that is weird is there's something in there. It's made of stone so worn you can't tell anymore whether it was carved by somebody or if it's just a natural freak of time and water. Whatever it is, it sits in one wall of the cave, half-covered with seaweed, this thing, this face: half god, half ogre, with a broad snout, a frowning knotted brow, thick meaty lips, and heavy closed eyes. The waves that never stop moving touch its lips, withdraw, and come back to touch them again and wear them away. So worn. So old.

Nobody's scared of this face. It's not supposed to be evil or anything. But nobody knows anything about it either: how it got there or what it's supposed to be. And since the water in the cave is shallow you can walk right up and touch that face, if you want. I never wanted to, myself. Because even though I thought it wasn't evil or anything, like the bay outside the Grotto, it was sometimes in my nightmares.

As I climbed over the rocks that morning, all of Devil's Bay was in plain sight. I looked first to make sure there was no dead body lying on the sand that day. There wasn't, so I went on down the beach. By that time, I knew where I was headed and what I had to do.

I stopped when I got to the Needle, this stone shaft that stands maybe thirty feet high in the water. All around its base are smaller boulders. I stood there for a while and looked at all the sharp white barnacles on it and at the slimy seaweed that grew on its base and floated on the water around it. Then I looked up to its top and couldn't believe what I was about to do. And as I stood there and waited to begin doing it, my two selves who had been fairly quiet up until then began this big argument that went something like this:

"You're not thinking of climbing that, are you?"

"I sure am and when I get to the top (my brass band playing furiously to drown out all objections) I'm going to jump off."

"You're crazy. You're right off the wall."

"I'm going to do it."

"Jump off? So you can land on those rocks below? And then lie there bleeding with a broken back, in agony, until the tide comes in to drown you and put you out of your misery?"

"I'm going to do it just the same."

"Nobody knows you're here. If you fall, there won't be anybody to help you."

"I'll be okay. I'll jump into the sinkhole. I'll miss the rocks. You know how deep that sinkhole is."

"Yeah, yeah, yeah. Sure, you will."

"All I have to do is aim carefully before I jump."

"Aim carefully? From up there? The Needle isn't even flat on top. And remember, you're going to be scared to death to begin with. So when you try to stand up, you'll lose your balance. You'll fall for sure. Come on, don't be stupid. Give up the whole idea. You never climbed all the way to the top. And you sure never jumped off. Probably nobody ever has."

"Probably not. And that's why I have to."

"Forget it. Go home before you kill yourself."

"I can't."

"Why not?"

"You know why not. I have to show whatever decides

those things what I'm willing to do to get my mom back. After I've done that—"

"If you're still alive—"

"Then I can ask—"

"Ask what?"

"Where the line is."

"There isn't any line."

"I can ask."

"Ask who? Not that thing in the cave? You're even more retarded than I thought you were."

"I'm going to do it anyway."

"You're totally insane."

We were still arguing like that as I walked into the water.

The Needle looked a lot taller than usual. It shot up into the sky, so tall I had to tilt my head back to see the top. I thought of my mom. I pulled off my sneakers and threw them on the sand above the waterline. Then I looked at them. One had its sole in the sand, one lay on its side. They reminded me of dogs with their tongues hanging out, sort of patient and pathetic as they sat on the beach like that, with limp shoelaces and wrinkled sides, waiting for me to come back and put them on. And I wondered if I would ever wear them again.

I took one last look around, drew a deep breath because my heart was already trying to beat its way out of my chest, and began to climb. The first thing I did was cut my hand on some barnacles, just to prove to myself how nervous I was. I looked at the thin red line that crossed my palm like a razor cut and saw it start to bleed. I knew when I cut myself like that, I wasn't going to make it. That if I made it to the top at all, when I got there I would slip and fall. I saw it all: how I would lose my balance, waver wildly back and forth for one horrible instant and then just fall to the rocks below. So I turned up the brass band until it was deafening, quit thinking, and kept on climbing. I grabbed one handhold after another and was really careful, but never stopped going higher and higher.

Near the top I almost fell. And that moment was truly horrible. I quit breathing when it happened. My insides went all jellylike and sort of rushed out to grip the rock I pressed against. A breeze came and dried the cold sweat that came out of my face. I felt for a better grip and almost threw up. When I could move at all, I started to climb again. I had to. It was just as dangerous to go down as up. So there was nothing else I could do.

I don't know how long I sat on the top when I got there. It was probably quite a while, though, because I was way too scared to stand up. Being there was like being on top of a high building or something. And I knew that when I stood up, there would be nothing to hold onto but air. When I thought of really doing it—standing up, I mean—and then jumping into the water, my knees began to dance and I knew I couldn't do it. I was scared to look down, but I finally did.

The beach looked like it was a million miles away. When I looked down at it, the whole idea of getting my mom back by jumping off the Needle faded away and turned into a childish, stupid dream. And I thought nobody but somebody as dumb as I would have even thought of doing such an impossible thing.

But then I thought of Excalibur: another impossible thing. And knew that since he existed nothing was really impossible anymore. I thought of my mom in that huge room waiting patiently for me to come get her. Then I stood up, very slowly and carefully, to keep my balance. I thought of Excalibur again. I looked down at the sinkhole. My heart was pounding so hard I could scarcely breathe. I thought of my mom. Then, before I could think anything else or argue with myself any longer, I jumped.

And what happened after that was horrible, horrible, horrible. I fell through space. The world flew past me like some vast disaster. The beach shot up to kill me. There was just time to think I was finished, that I'd made my worst and final mistake, that my life was over, before I hit the water. I touched the sand at the bottom of the sinkhole, I died and I lived again all in about five seconds, before I surfaced.

I crawled out of the water. I lay facedown on the sand. I hadn't crashed on the rocks or been killed, but I was in a million pieces all the same. And I couldn't believe I'd actually jumped. I could not believe it. Even now, whenever I think of it, I don't know how I did it.

And all I can say about it is, except for not being killed outright, the whole thing was just as bad as I thought it would be. And I sure knew I'd never do it again.

It took a while to pull myself together. I just lay on the sand until I did. But once I had, I started to feel a lot better.

I had these long red lines of barnacle cuts on my hands and feet. And my clothes were heavy with water, but after I wrung them out the air wasn't too cold or anything. And by the time I walked over to pick up my sneakers I was feeling pretty pleased with myself. It seemed like a long time since I'd thrown them there on the sand.

I began to feel really good as I walked down the beach away from the Needle—all in one piece—because I'd done what I said I would. I'd kept a promise and was sure that whatever kept track of such things must've noticed. And that was why the brass band started up again and was going full blast when I got to the Grotto. Because I was so sure I'd already earned my reward. All I would have to do was ask that face inside it another impossible thing—and it would tell me. It was as easy as that. I was pretty sure my mom and I would be home in time for dinner. I could hardly wait to see Stan's face.

The Grotto hadn't changed since the last time I saw it. It was still all rock, all darkness and restless moving water. The same distant cannon boomed somewhere deep inside it. The same voices wept, whispered, gurgled, laughed, and moaned in the water there. And all the things you can almost but not quite remember; yellow eyes and the music that was behind the sound of water, the goat smell, a horned head, and then the first sight of that blind, ancient face that just completely wiped out my brass band.

I walked on until I was up to my knees in water and stood before the face. I stared at it. Nothing happened. It kept its eyes closed. I didn't move. I asked my question. Nothing happened. I asked again. It didn't answer. It didn't move. I waited and closed my eyes. I hoped and wished and asked again. The only answer was the sound of moving water.

And that was when I knew once and for all that the Grotto wasn't my cave, all filled with light. It was nothing, just empty darkness; no gods, no secrets, and no oracles were there. It was just nothing. And the face inside it was nothing too, mindless as the waves that touched its lips. Nothing like Excalibur could've lived inside the Grotto for a single instant.

I waited for a little longer for something to happen. I wasn't too surprised, though, when nothing did. Just sort of embarrassed. I mean, I felt sort of stupid to have thought a place like the Grotto could've had a thing to do with somebody like my mom. And being where I was and talking to a stone and everything and wishing somebody like the girl I always passed in the hall after second period had seen me jump off the Needle.

I might have given up the whole idea of finding my mom right then and there forever, if it hadn't been for Excalibur. But I couldn't forget the night of my birthday, how trapped and miserable I'd been. How I called for help. How right after that I'd found Excalibur was the answer to my call— an impossible thing, which pointed to some enormous fact I didn't yet understand, but which made me think there might be a lot of other things out there that nobody under-stood.

So I didn't give up. I thought that even if the Grotto was a big mistake, I'd find that line between life and death yet. Maybe even that very day. I was sure there had to be some good reason why I was there at Devil's Bay that morning.

Then, an instant later, I thought that maybe I knew what it was. Because I stopped dead where I was and felt the hairs rise on my head. I mean, they really did. They rose at the roots like somebody's hair in a comic strip, because I looked out at the Devil's Finger where it pointed to the ocean. And away in the distance, far out in the sea mist, where the waves leaped and fell back into themselves and leaped again in this wild death dance that had no beginning and no end—away out there, this small black figure stood.

Some fog had started to roll in from the ocean and anyway, the figure was too far away to see clearly. But the first thing I thought was, it was something or somebody I might not want to see more clearly. Or come any closer to.

In my mind I crossed the beach and went up to it, where it stood with its back to me in the fog. When it heard me it wheeled around fast to face me. And its face was the white face with the red lipsticked mouth of the dead girl with the rag around her neck. Or something else even worse, maybe, that I didn't even know about yet. Something that made me want to turn and run up the beach in the opposite direction as fast I could.

I didn't though. What I did was stop where I was and strain my eyes to see better. As I looked the fog began to come in faster, but that distant figure never moved. The fog seemed to make no difference to it. It seemed not to

97

notice. Which was weird because everybody knows how dangerous fog can be on the coast when the tide is coming in.

And from being scared of whoever was out there, I started to be scared *for* whoever was out there, instead. I even started to sort of worry. Because, I thought, what if it wasn't something weird or one of the dead who walked there at all? What if it was only a tourist, somebody who didn't know a thing about the Devil's Finger or even about the ocean? Somebody who thought it was perfectly safe and all right to stand there on a sandspit like that with the tide and fog rolling in?

8
Quicksand

The fog got thicker the closer I got to the Devil's Finger. As I ran I yelled to whoever it was who stood there, but the wind snatched up my voice and mixed it with the sound of the waves and the gulls' screams before it tossed it into the air again, so nobody could hear me.

As I came closer still, I could see the white foam on top of the waves as they crested, roared, and hurled themselves on the beach. I knew those waves: they would break in clear, circular washes at the foot of the person standing there, each with a swirl of bubbles at the edge. I thought how the water would come in and out, in and out, so that whoever stood and looked down at it would be fascinated and stay to watch, half hypnotized, while the sandspit became an island that got smaller and smaller—with quicksand in the channel behind it and the raging ocean in front. Until at last. . . .

I crossed from the mainland to the sandspit on the last piece of solid ground, and was close enough to see I'd been right to worry as I had. Because it wasn't one of the dead or anything weird at all. It was just a little kid, probably about five years old.

By that time the tide was running fast in the channel behind me and the fog was thicker than before. All the same, I still had time for some pretty weird thoughts about him after I saw his face. It wasn't one you'd see just any old time. Not at all. It was bright, cold, unearthly. Something made from mist and the wild roar of the ocean. A merchild's face. He was real, though. He had on jeans and sneakers. But no shirt, so you could see how thin he was, with little chicken ribs and sharp shoulder blades and goose bumps on his arms.

It was really strange to see such a little kid out there all alone on that beach where nobody else would go for anything. He didn't seem surprised to see me. He just smiled this little kid smile. Then he said, "Hi." He had the sweet, high voice little kids always have.

"I was wondering," he said calmly, "how I was going to get back."

He didn't look worried at all, though. But I was sure worried. I knew about fog. It could be so dense on the beach that you could be completely turned around in it. Instead of heading inland, like you thought, you could walk straight into the ocean and be caught by the tide.

"We can still make it," I said, "but we'll have to move fast."

He looked at the channel. It was already wide but the water that rushed in was only about two feet deep.

"It's not too deep to wade."

"No," I said, "but there's quicksand in it."

He had big eyes, the kind with light behind them so

that they really shone. When I said that, they got bigger and a scared look came into them. I'd been about to mention the car I knew about that was buried in the quicksand in that channel: some teenage kids had parked it on the sand and gone to climb the bluff. Meanwhile the tide came in and they got back just in time to see it go down under the sand. But I decided not to. He was just a little kid. He looked scared enough already.

"There is?" As he spoke, a muffled sound like the death moan of a wounded giant filled the air around us, louder than the waves. When it stopped, another long, drawn-out, sad and warning call came from farther down the coast. The fog was serious that day, they said, and dangerous. If we waited much longer we might not make it back at all.

"What are we going to do?" Though he tried not to, he looked ready to cry.

"Move fast," I said.

"Move fast where?"

"Across the channel," I said, now the complete man of action: cool as ice, steely eyed, and just about as scared as he was. But the way he looked at me when I said it certainly didn't hurt anything. And though I was scared to death and not sure what might happen, all the same, I could see a fairly cool moment rolling up over the horizon for me. And even though I thought it might very well be my last moment, I still couldn't help sort of looking forward to it all the same.

"But what about the quicksand?" he asked in a thin, breathless little voice.

The cool moment had arrived.

"I know the path through it," Super Hero Olmstead said superbly.

It felt pretty neat to say it like that. And when I did, he looked at me just the way somebody ought to look at somebody who'd just said something like that. It felt so good, in fact, that since he was a lot younger than I was and there was nobody like Stan around to overhear me say it and laugh, I even added another line: "Trust me," I said. "I'll get us through." I was glad nobody else was there when I said it, though, and right afterward I almost got one of those big, guilty grins on my face: you know, the kind you get when you've just embarrassed even yourself? But I didn't because underneath it all, I really was too scared to smile. It had been a long time since I'd walked the path through the quicksand. I wasn't sure I remembered it. I was scared, too, that it might have shifted or something. And with quicksand you weren't allowed even one mistake. But we had no choice either. It was move or drown.

"Come on," I said. I took his hand.

"No," he said. "I'm scared."

"Come on," I said in this voice that was anything but cool by that time. "We've got to move."

He pulled away, so I gave him this little shake and tried to look at him the way Captain Kirk of the *Enterprise* would have under the same circumstances.

"Now you listen good," I said and tried to sound like Kirk would've if it had been him and not me on that sandspit, "and do what I tell you. When I start out, you walk behind me. Walk exactly where I walk. Don't take a step until you're sure your foot will be exactly where mine was."

He was nothing but a pair of big, worried eyes.

"Make one mistake, and you're dead," I said.

I only wanted to show him how serious it was. The minute I said it though, I saw I'd made a big mistake. He began to cry.

"I'm not going," he said.

"You have to."

"No."

Because the tide and fog came in so fast, I was truly scared we might not make it through the channel at all. I didn't grab him or anything though. I just held out my hand.

"Come on," I said. "We'll be okay. I know the way."

But he held out his arms to be carried instead, so I picked him up. He wasn't too heavy. I thought I could make it. I watched the seawater rush through the channel and thought something like this:

I'm all Excalibur has. There must be a reason why I found him and not somebody else. It was no accident. And it was no accident I found this little kid either. I'm all he's got, too, right now. I've got to get across this channel and not be caught in quicksand. So I'm calling you, whatever you are. You helped me in the cave on my birthday night so please help me now.

Whatever it was, I think it heard me. Because that

quiet I'd felt in the cave that night came again and settled all around me, so that I didn't feel afraid anymore or feel anything but just held in that golden stillness. Then the sound of the waves came back, I felt the weight of the little kid in my arms again and the fog in my face as I stepped into the channel.

Once I started, I remembered what to look for, so the way through it was clear. Once, right in the middle, I nearly panicked because for one second I couldn't remember where to step. But the little kid's breath that came all warm on my neck reminded me how much he trusted me to get us across. So I made myself stop being all that scared. And once I stopped being totally petrified and went back to just being worried, the way through the channel was clear to me again.

We made it across to the mainland just in time. The sandspit where we'd stood before was entirely under water and hidden behind a wall of white fog. Down the coast a foghorn moaned again and warned anybody on the beach how bad the weather was.

"Come on," I said. "We're not safe yet. We can still get lost in this fog. We've got to get to the dunes."

He didn't say anything. He just followed me up the beach, away from the ocean toward the foot of the bluff.

9
Gareth

We sat down on the sand with our backs against a log and looked for a while at the ferns and trees that grew on the bluff—anywhere but at the ocean. We didn't talk at first. We just rested and looked each other over—secretly, so as not to be rude about it or anything—because that was the first chance we had to see what we looked like out of the fog.

We tried not to catch each other at it. Every time I looked at him, though, I wanted to look again, because he had these weird, neat eyes. They were sea eyes: green, the color of beach glass and clear as water. And every time he looked at me they said the same thing: how strong and smart and fearless I was. *El Coolo,* in a word. Nobody in my whole life had ever looked at me like that. It felt pretty good. In fact, terrific.

Except for his eyes, though, once we were out of the fog and I could see him better, there was nothing startling to him. I thought he looked about the way a little kid his age ought to look: sort of unsuspecting and happy and, I guess, innocent is the word. Like somebody whose thoughts were still the kind you have when you're that little: all bright and weirdly pleasant, like soap bubbles shot up from a blue earth into a green sky. With maybe a dark side to them, but still pretty free from all the garbage you collect in your head when you're older. . . .

As I said, we didn't talk at first. It was good just to be safe again where it was quiet, with all the bad stuff over. Except for down at the water's edge, the fog had burned off, so that the sky was higher; but the sky and sand were still this soft, comfortable gray. Where we sat smelled like bitter green and sweet rot—like seaweed on rocks—with a passing scent of Christmas every so often from the pines on the bluff. It was just so nice to be there. I can't tell you. I could've stayed all day. Or maybe forever. I asked him what his name was.

"Gareth Morgan," he said.

I asked where he lived.

He said he lived on another beach over that way, and pointed.

On a boat. (I knew the boat. There really was one.)

"With three of his friends," he said, "from outer space." He didn't know their names. He thought one of them might be called Web Man because he'd spun a web to live in across one corner of the boat. But he didn't think the others even had names. They all had phasers though, that shot out red lethal beams that could even penetrate deflector shields. (For such a little kid he had this really terrific vocabulary.) They never hurt people though. They only destroyed bad robots. And they were all so nice. They liked him a lot. They were his only friends, he said.

What about the kids at school?

He said he didn't go to school. His mommy taught him at home. She was a mermaid.

"A mermaid?" I asked.

"*Once*," he said. But not anymore. He bet I couldn't guess what he wanted for his birthday.

I said I couldn't.

Either a baby seal or a little pig. He didn't care which.

I said maybe his dad would get him one.

He said he didn't think he would because his dad was dead. Killed a long time ago by a gorilla.

"A gorilla? In a jungle?" I asked.

"Not in a jungle. In a civil war," he said. He wanted a baby pig because his mommy said pigs were very smart. "So I could teach it tricks," he said. But then if he had a baby seal he could go swimming with it. He could keep it on the boat with Web Man and the others. So it would be close to the ocean. He would feed it seaweed instead of fish, though, because fish had feelings, too. I said rats were nice to have for pets because they were smart and affectionate and that I'd had one once.

He wanted to know what its name was.

I said her name was Lulu.

He laughed. He said it was a funny name for a rat and that it was a better mouse name. . . .

Did I like root beer? *He* did.

I said, "Who doesn't?"

Did I know the song about the old woman who

swallowed a fly? Every time he heard it, it made him feel sick. Especially the part about the spider. That wiggled and jiggled inside her? It *was* a pretty sickening song come to think of it.

Then I said, "With a fish tail?" Because my mind ran a little behind his.

"Who?" he asked.

"Your mom. The mermaid. Did she have a fish tail?"

He said, sure she did. In the carnival. She pulled it up over her legs. Then she sat up on this high platform and people threw tennis balls at her. If they hit her she fell off into the water and they got a prize. But that was before he was born, in the time of the ancient Egyptians. Did I know about Osiris? Horus was his favorite. Did I like potato chips? *He* did. He said he'd gone to Devil's Bay that morning to look for baby seals. He'd thought there might be some on the sandspit but he hadn't found any. All he'd found on the beach were a few mermaids, the kind you had to give faces to, and a poor little dead mouse.

So then I knew who'd made the three weird sisters, those demented looking guardians of the beach I'd found propped up against the rocks that day. I told him he sure knew how to make good mermaids. He wagged his head in agreement, pleased.

While he said all that stuff I sort of leaned back against my log and closed my eyes to hear better, because the conversation we were having was sort of like his eyes: neat and weird at the same time, the kind I liked best. It just freewheeled around and went nowhere in particular with several stops in outer space on the way and was full of nice, unexpected impossible things. Where you could sit someplace like I was and listen to forever.

A blue butterfly danced over our heads. You could still hear the hollow roar of the ocean but only when the wind was right. We sat there on the sand and he told me some more about Web Man and the gorilla that lived in the civil war. And why it might be good to be friends with a Venusian. I let sand run through my fingers and listened and thought that if I ever told anybody about Excalibur, he would probably be the right one and maybe the only one to tell. Because he would've believed me instantly and completely. And be unsurprised.

He asked if I could come home with him. Then closed his eyes, held his breath, and put his hands over his ears so he wouldn't hear if I said "no."

"Did you mean to the boat? With Web Man and everybody?" I asked.

No, to his red house. Where his mommy was. "Could you?" he asked.

Something, maybe what had almost happened to him already that day, made me want to see that he got all the way home, that his mom was where she was supposed to be, and that he was safe for sure. It was only a little past noon. There was still plenty of time to see Excalibur. So I said, sure I could. He let out the breath he held.

Where was his house?

He pointed south where there was nothing but the far

dunes and the Andersen house. Then, when he did that, that was when I knew who he was. And what to think of him.

As for his mom, the mermaid, I'd never actually seen her myself, but I knew what to think about her too. I knew all about her and where she lived and that she had this little kid. Because every so often somebody would say something ought to be done about him, that a woman like that shouldn't be allowed to have a kid out there in the far dunes where nobody could see how he was treated or what went on. Though since he was hers, he was probably as strange and weird as she was by that time and beyond all human help anyway; not that he was mentioned all that often, because it was the mermaid people were interested in. She was the one they were really after.

I never heard that she bothered anybody. She just kept to herself and never went to places like Fat George's or Nelson's supermarket or any place where other people were. Everybody knew how she got her food, though. My second cousin, Chris Bjornsen, delivered her groceries to her twice a month in his pickup. But that was the only thing everybody knew about her for sure.

Which was sort of fatal, because what people didn't know about her they began to make up and pretty soon everybody knew all kinds of things about her. All bad. In fact, you wouldn't believe the stuff they said. Like for instance that there were some remote beaches way down to the south and certain places in the woods, I mean deep woods, where somebody or other would say they'd seen her. At first, all they'd say was they'd seen her there. But then, later on, they'd wonder out loud to anybody they met what she could be doing in a lonely place like that, where she'd no business to be, since she never dug for clams or hunted deer? Then later people began to tell each other about this sack she carried with her, this big burlap bag, when she went to those lonely places. And wonder what was in the bag, because something moved in there, they said, as if something were alive and trying to get out—and had they ever found that little girl who was missing up Moon Creek way? That the whole thing was pretty damn peculiar. And that maybe the reason she lived so far out and liked to be alone so much was because she knew more than she ought to about things no human being had any right to know anything about at all. And did things she wouldn't want anyone else to see.

And so, it wasn't too long before everybody around here knew for sure that on moonless nights the dead went to the Andersen house to call on her and pay their respects. And that when she walked on the sandspit at Devil's Bay, she never walked alone, but arm-in-arm with the drowned who'd haunt that beach . . . that when the moon was full she danced naked on the beach and that this black shadow of a horned man that was larger than life danced with her.

Stan had never seen her any more than I had. He talked about her sometimes, though, like whenever we heard a new story about her. And when we did, Stan always said her big crime was that she chose to live as far away from everybody as she could get. And that nobody could forgive her for keeping to herself that way.

He also said that where she lived and what was said about her had all the makings of something that could be truly bad. Because, he said, women like her were like stray cats—and people might let a cat live under their porch for a while and leave it alone, the way they let her live out there in the Andersen house without doing anything about it. But all the same, nobody liked her any the better for being something that was beautiful and independent and harmless anymore than they liked the cat for being these things. And like the cat, everybody knew how easy it would be to hunt her down whenever they felt like it. That maybe because she lived in a place that was hard to get to or because most of the people forgot she was there, they just hadn't got around to it yet. But one of these days, Stan said, somebody would go out there. Because there was always somebody around who liked to hunt cats. And it was too bad, but there wasn't a thing anybody could to about it either, because there was nothing definite to warn her about. But all the same, it was probably just a matter of time, he said, until something ugly happened out there, because that was how people were. Which was, Stan said, one of the many reasons he personally wished he was a tree or cabbage or something else that was unthreatening and respectable. Anything at all, in fact, so long as it wasn't human.

When I asked him if he believed any of the stories about her, he just laughed and said he believed them all because they were too gorgeously stupid not to believe. Good old Stan. In some ways he never let me down.

I laughed with him when he said that, but secretly I sort of wanted to believe those stories all the same. I thought they were neat. Besides, it was pretty hard to believe they were not true. So I did believe them, at least some of them, anyway.

By the time I finished thinking this, we were in the woods up on the bluff where it's so quiet that if you speak at all, it has to be in whispers because it always feels like something—maybe it's the trees—listens to what you say in there.

We didn't say anything at all though. We just walked along. Gareth hummed a wordless, endless little tune to himself as we went. The path was really narrow so I walked behind him. I looked down at the top of his head as it sort of bobbed along ahead of me and thought about the something ugly Stan was so sure would happen some day. I made up my mind that whatever it was, it was not going to happen to him, because I wouldn't let it. I had no idea how I could stop it. I only knew fiercely from the top of my head right down to the soles of my sneakers and with all my mind and everything I had, that I would. And as we walked along the path through the woods I silently promised him that if it took the last drop of blood and the last breath in my body, Stan's "Something Ugly" would never happen. And once I did that, I felt better and not so worried about everything anymore.

And then—right that second—right after I promised

myself, was when I got my big insight, brilliant as a neon sign that suddenly went on in my head and made everything that mattered stand out bold and clear as if a million hot blue arrows pointed in that direction. I mean, important stuff like why I'd really been at Devil's Bay that morning: which was not to risk my life to prove to whoever handles those things what I was willing to do to get my mom back, like I'd thought it was. And for sure not to ask some stupid old stone image—as a desperate last resort—how to do it either.

The real reason why I was at Devil's Bay that day was because I was sent there. I didn't know who sent me. You can't know everything. Some things nobody knows. But I sure knew why. In the first place, it was to save somebody from being drowned in the ocean. In the second place, it was to keep somebody from being hurt by something ugly. But what was even more—and about here the meaning of the whole thing ran through me like a half pleasant, half deadly electric shock—this somebody I'd been sent to help wasn't just anybody. This somebody's mother was supposed to walk with the dead. And if that were true, if she really did, then, I thought, she would have to know more about them than anybody else. So if there really were such a thing as a line between life and death that could be crossed, she was probably the only one who could tell me where it was and how to cross it. If she wanted to. And she would probably want to, considering what I'd done that day. The more I thought about it, the more it seemed it was something that was meant to be. Like fate or something.

Because it was so perfect and complete, so much the answer I'd been looking for when I came to the beach that day, I believed it must be another impossible thing that happened to me, like finding Excalibur. I thought that nothing that happened that day happened by chance. I was there that morning to save Gareth. And he was there to save me.

By the time I reached the end of this big insight, we'd passed the place where there are always about a million blackberries in August and were in the far dunes. We could hear the ocean again and when we turned south I knew for sure I'd been right about who he was and where he lived because the Andersen house was the only house in that direction.

It sat by itself smack in the middle of nowhere, painted red on the outside because the Andersens are Swedes and red is the color Swedes paint their country houses.

I knew it pretty well. I used to sleep over pretty often when Eric Andersen lived there. I hadn't seen it for a long time, though.

When we got to it, I saw it hadn't changed. It was still red. The same picket fence leaned in, then out, then wandered crazily all around the house where it sat in the sand for no very good reason. The same Andersen path all lined with clamshells led up to it. The only thing that was different about it was the mermaid who stood on the front porch.

Everybody always said she was good-looking, but all the same, I hadn't expected her to be *that* good-looking.

What I mean is, she wasn't just good-looking. She was *really* good-looking. What I'm trying to say is: there are people who a few other people think are good-looking. And there are people who are good-looking sometimes, in certain ways, if that's the kind of look you like. There are all the people who think they're a lot better looking than they really are. And then there are the ones like Gareth's mom, who are just so good-looking the way a beautiful bird's egg or seashell or a ripe plum is: something that just looks so neat and complete, you want to take it home with you to keep forever just to have to look at.

Which would've been okay, except that how she looked made it pretty hard for me to connect her with what they said about her, even at the start. I'd expected somebody good-looking all right, but in a different way, with maybe smoldering eyes and black snaky hair, or something. I know that's childish, but that's how I imagined her all the same.

Once the first shock was over though, I got myself together and thought, who was I to say how somebody like her was supposed to look? After all, there was no law that said she had to look like a refugee from *Chiller Theater*. If she really was totally weird or supernatural or something, she probably would be too smart to advertise it by looking that way. Poisonous things could look beautiful and harmless, too, sometimes. Take that toadstool called "The Angel of Death." Pure white inside and out. Beautiful. So you couldn't see how bad it was. At least, that's how I figured it.

No matter how hard I tried though, I couldn't feel really good about it. The way she looked, I mean. And the way she acted didn't make me feel any better. She was terrible. I mean, here was somebody who was supposed to be really weird, really strange and all. Now you don't think of somebody like that as ever getting all excited or glad or too upset about anything, do you? Of course not. People like that are cold and calm and deadly all the time. They don't go jumping off porches or rushing up to anybody the way normal people do—the way *she* did—the instant she caught sight of us. Or act so foolishly glad just to see one little kid, even if he is her own. Not at all. They're too icy and evil and everything to do stuff like that.

I wasn't ready to give her up altogether though. I still had some faith left in my big insight. I realized I didn't know much about the kind of weirdness she was supposed to have. But I thought I could find out. So I decided to go slow: just to watch her very carefully that day, and not say much, but keep a sharp lookout for any signs of what she was—like things she said or stuff I might see around the house. The thing was, I'd already made so many mistakes in the way I'd gone about trying to get my mom back that I'd sort of lost faith in myself. I was really anxious to do everything right, because in a way, I thought this was probably my last chance to find her. So I thought I must just be careful and watch Gareth's mom. Then later, if I thought she was enough of what they said she was for me to depend on, I would decide what to do next.

Before she could actually say a word herself, though, Gareth started to tell her where he'd been and go on about mermaids and baby seals. But mostly about what had been the main event that morning: namely me, as the super hero. And right away, I mean, the minute he started to tell her, everything went from bad to worse. At least, from my point of view. Because even before he got to the part where I saved him from the ocean, she began to give me these looks. Not that they weren't nice, because they were: all grateful and everything. But of course the thing was, I didn't want them. In fact, each time I got one, it practically destroyed me. Because if you're trying to convince yourself somebody is pure evil or something, looks like that can really do you in. Plus the fact that her eyes were exactly like Gareth's: the kind you could look right into without being afraid because there was nothing to hurt you there. I told myself she kept her eyes that way on purpose to hide what she was really like. So nobody would suspect what she did at night when the moon was full. It helped a little, but not much.

Anyway, Gareth talked to us all the way into the Andersen house. Which smelled as damp and spidery inside as ever, and looked the way it had when the Andersens lived there: kind of beach-shacky and bare, with no curtains on the windows and all the wobbly old Andersen furniture still standing around.

It was kind of messed up in there, too, but in a cheerful sort of way. There was a pile of chewed up looking kids' books on the floor with some comics, the kind you get in thrift stores. You know, *Richie Rich*, *Little Lotta*, *Casper the Friendly Ghost*. Some toys, mostly trucks and stuffed animals. Somebody's shell collection was lined up on all the windowsills and on a rickety Andersen table there were some crayons, a hunk of clay, and an open book.

I knew that book. It was one we had at home. Which is a lot more astonishing than it sounds. You just never see any books Stan reads in anybody else's house. Most people have never even heard of the books Stan likes. But there it was, facedown on the table. And what was even more amazing, on the shelf of books against the wall I saw another. It was pretty disappointing not to see even one book on magic or the occult or anything like that though. There was nothing like that at all. In fact there was nothing my Grampa Olmstead could've made a fuss about. So I started to feel destroyed all over again, but then I caught myself and sort of reasoned that if you were somebody who was already able to stroll down the beach arm-in-arm with the dead and dance with horned shadows, to say nothing of all the rest, you were, you might say, already there. You wouldn't need a pile of how-to books. At least, that's how I explained it to myself at the time.

Once Gareth finished what he had to say, she said her name was Gwen Morgan and went on to tell me what she thought of me and what I'd done that morning. It was fairly cool the way she put it: in fact, I probably could've stood there and listened forever. It'd been a pretty long time since anybody had said something like that to me right to my face that way. In fact, I couldn't remember the last time it had happened, if ever. But there she stood and turned that bare room into a golden place just by being there, and told me how super-wonderful I was. As moments go, that one was fairly cool, all right. On the other hand, as far as being somebody who rubbed shoulders with evil on a regular basis went, she began to look like a total loss. There was no getting around it. She messed up every time.

Take the quicksand for instance: whenever she remembered it she grabbed Gareth and held him close. With this look on her face that was anything but like what I hoped she was. I liked to see her do it, though, even if it did make me feel bad at the same time and miss my own mom more than ever. And even though it sort of messed up my hopes of her being somebody who could help me, I didn't want her to stop doing it, because when she did, they looked so nice together.

Anyhow, whether I liked it or not, there wasn't a thing I could do about it. So I told myself that maybe in spite of everything she'd said and done so far and in spite of how she looked, it might still be all right. That my big insight was still worth something and not just another one of my stupid mistakes. That it was just possible people with forbidden knowledge liked their kids the way ordinary people did. And that maybe—maybe—they didn't always have to act weird or look weird to be weird.

So that was where I was when I saw how late it was getting and thought of Excalibur waiting for me in the cave and said I had to go.

"Don't go," Gareth said.

I said I had to.

"Then come back tomorrow."

I said maybe I would.

She just smiled at me and looked all beautiful and asked me how she could ever thank me enough.

I wanted to tell her but I didn't dare. Not yet. I was too scared she might not even know what I was talking about. And if she didn't, I didn't want to know she didn't. I wanted to keep up my hopes a little longer.

And anyhow, I was really confused at the time. I told myself if so many people knew all those stories about her, then some of them had to be true. But on the other hand, she didn't seem. . . . I just didn't know. I just didn't know what to think.

But all the same, as I walked away from that crazy picket fence that so carefully shut out sand from sand, as I yelled good-bye back to Gareth for about the ninetieth time, I thought I would ask her anyway the next time I saw her, no matter what. Because it was all I could think to do, all I really had left to do.

All the way down the beach I planned how I'd do it, what I'd say and what she'd say back. I didn't quit until I was over the Dogs, until I was actually in the cave and saw Excalibur.

He sure wasn't hard to find. He was at the back of the cave, standing over his nest. He'd grown again overnight and was roughly the size of an elephant. He dwarfed his nest. He towered over me. All gleaming bronze and gold and emerald as he was, with fires blazing in wonderful eyes; he didn't look helpless and he didn't look trapped. When I saw him like that, all my worries disappeared, for a moment anyway. I just stood there staring and admiring and hardly believing my eyes, the way you do when you see something truly beautiful: glad to be there, able to see him, and that it's you and not somebody else, who might want to spoil or change him.

In twenty-four hours everything about him had changed. He stood upright all the time now. Besides being larger, he looked a lot stronger too, and the monstrous, beautiful brute that moved like a stranger behind the smoky gold surface of his face had grown clearer, more compelling and mysterious. I don't know what or who it was behind there, but some of what I saw of it was disturbing. Something was there that was—not exactly terrible, not exactly dangerous, but all the same . . .

He seemed happy to see me though. He stayed where he was and watched me with his beautiful eyes until I came up close to him. I had a smooth, white, cookie-shaped stone in my hand. He took it delicately with his long blue tongue and crunched it to dust. He always ate everything I offered him just because I offered it. And I gave it to him not because I thought he was hungry, but because I wanted to see if his teeth had grown. They had, all three sets. They looked razor sharp. I shivered a little just looking at them. I wondered why he had such terrible teeth and claws?

He didn't know. Did he need them?

I didn't know why he should ask *me*. I thought about it seriously, though, and after deep consideration thought he did because the world outside the cave was cruel.

If he ever got outside the cave, he would need all the help he could get.

. . . then that was why he had them.

What had changed the most since the day before were his wings. They had been stumpy little things, like something that belonged on a fledgling. They had grown overnight, changed shape, and turned from gray to smoky gold. There were dim patterns beginning to show on them too, which I could barely see yet, just as I couldn't make out the shape they were becoming because Excalibur kept them folded at his sides. I kept wishing he would open them or resettle or even flap them like birds do just once so I could see his wingspan, but he didn't.

He couldn't. They weren't ready yet.

Would he fly someday?

Would he?

How would I know?

I knew. I knew everything about him, if I would only think about it. Those wings weren't for nothing. So I thought he probably would. I sat down on the white sand beach. He came and sat close beside me, like always, as if he liked my company; only now he towered over my head, so after a moment he lay down on the sand beside me. He closed his eyes. His eyelids were blue, the color and texture of sheet metal.

This time, though, it wasn't as peaceful sitting there

with him as it had been before, because I started to worry again. What if something happened to me, I thought, what if I broke a leg climbing back over the rocks? What would happen to him? Would he wait and then finally leave the cave to look for me? And if he kept on growing at his present rate, it would be terrible when he did break out.

I could see it all, like one of those Japanese sci-fi films: people running down the beach like panicked ants, with Excalibur, bigger than Godzilla, bigger than King Kong, out there looking for me: confused, helpless—the perfect target. They wouldn't even try to catch him. By that time they'd just be afraid and want to kill him. And they would, too, after hunting him down and scaring him. *Talk about being depressed!* I sat there for a long time in total gloom, worrying, with Excalibur lying about six inches from my left sneaker, as I thought that if he went out there, he would never survive.

He was perfectly safe. There was nothing that could hurt him, ever.

Yeah, that was fine. But he'd never seen a helicopter armed with a machine gun or tear gas. No, they wouldn't hurt him: they'd just kill him.

Not to worry. He lived under universal law. He was immortal.

Maybe so, but all the same, if he went out of the cave, he'd never make it back alive, towering over the dunes like that.

Then why had I made him so big?

Made him? Made him? He always talked in riddles.

It wasn't a riddle. Hadn't he already told me he wasn't limited to one shape like I was? That the rules he lived under were different from mine? That ought to be enough. If I thought about it I ought to be able to figure out the rest myself. It was all stuff I already knew and had just forgotten.

I was never any good at puzzles though. And it was getting dark. So, though I hated to, I had to tear myself away from Excalibur and the cave. I said good-bye and that I'd see him tomorrow. I left him on the white sand beach.

10
Letters

There was a bad-news letter addressed to Dr. Troy Straw-bridge lying in wait for me when I got up the next morning. It was on the living room floor where Stan had probably dropped it after she gave it to him. I figured it had to do with me because it was from some place called Applegate Village School. The envelope was open so I looked inside.

There was a brochure with a load of you-know-what in it about how this school, up in "the healthful mountains of Vermont," was a "special place for special people, a dif-ferent kind of learning experience where individuality is cherished." Translated, the whole thing meant that it was too far up in the ice and snow for any wackos who were sent there to be able to get away into town and cause any trouble. At least, that was how I read it, and the picture on the front of the brochure bore me out. It was of this stringy haired girl with a serious eating problem—I mean she was huge—leaning over this weedy looking wimp—a burn-out, if I ever saw one—pretending to look into a microscope, while this hippie looking old guy, obviously faculty, looked on and pretended to be interested. Apple-gate Village School. Wow. Yuck. That brochure didn't fool me for one minute. I hoped it wouldn't fool Stan either. I stood there and looked at it for a while and tried to decide which I thought was worse: Applegate Village School or Stoneygate Military Academy. I couldn't choose, though. Each was sort of perfect in its own awful way.

I was so busy thinking that stuff I didn't hear Stan come into the room. But before I could put down the brochure, there he was, standing right beside me. He looked like he was in a good mood.

"What ho," he said, which was the way he talked sometimes when he was feeling good. "What giveth?"

"Not much," I said. It was a pretty straight and stupid thing to say, even considering the way I felt, but I couldn't think of anything better just then.

"Been reading my mail, I see," Stan said as he looked down at the envelope I held.

"You left it lying all over the floor," I said. "It sure looks like a horrible place."

"You think so?" He looked sort of disappointed.

"Yeah. Even worse than Stoneygate Military Academy." I looked him right in the eye when I said that. And old Stan looked amused. He had a pretty decent sense of humor sometimes.

"Where boys become—" he said. "Whatever. Like Randi."

"Yeah," I said. I decided to get a little tougher. "So what's happening? What was the 'something good' we had to talk about?"

"Oh, that." Stan looked at me with this funny little grin

I'd never seen on his face before. "Are you ready?"

"I guess so," I said. "Hit me with it. Get it over with."

"Okay," he said, "here goes." He straightened up and cleared his throat theatrically, while I watched him coldly. I could see he was going to make a production of it.

"Important announcement."

Man, was he ever corny. He practically said "ta da!" He tried to sound like a town crier or somebody but only slightly, not all the way, like he'd probably planned to, but because I looked too sarcastic, he lost his nerve.

"Well?" I said, "let's have it."

"Okay—uh—" he said. "Well here it is, the something good: Troy and I are getting hitched. We decided last night."

He looked anxious when he said it, like he was all prepared with smelling salts or something in case I should scream and faint. Actually, I did scream and faint when he said it, but only inside myself, where he couldn't see it.

"Congratulations." I was cold and ironic as anything, but he looked relieved anyway. He'd probably thought I'd throw a fit.

"When's the big day?"

"Fairly soon," he said. "We haven't really set it yet. But soon, fairly soon."

"I hope you'll be very happy," I said, all irony, all politeness. "And when are you planning to send me away?"

You could tell he hadn't expected me to say that, because he looked upset.

"Aw, come on," he said, "you know I'd never send you

away . . . not unless you wanted to go," he added. Craftily, I thought.

"Wanted to go?" I repeated. "To Stoneygate? To Applegate Village?"

"It might be interesting for a change," Stan said.

I took a good look at him when he said that and knew that, as far as I was concerned, it was hopeless; he was a zombie. She'd taken his mind away. The brainwashing job she'd done was too complete. He could say he wouldn't send me away to a boarding school unless I "wanted to go." Once they were married, Troy would see to it that I did want to go. Very, very much. I'd go all right. I'd probably beg to go. She had her little ways.

"Troy and I are going out to dinner tonight," Stan said. "Want to come along?"

But that would've been too much considering the shock of the news. And anyway, by that time I wasn't feeling all that good. In fact, it felt a lot like I'd just swallowed a rock and it was lying all hard and cold in the middle of my stomach, with another big rock to match it in my throat. I guess I must've looked pretty weird about then, because Stan looked at me as if he felt sorry for me or something, and said in this very nice way, "Don't worry so much about everything. It'll probably be all right, you know."

He reached out and sort of tried to tousle my hair or something, but I pulled my head away out of reach. He didn't really care how I felt. He just wanted the whole thing to be easy and no sweat for him. At least, that's what I thought. As far as I was concerned, the minute he said he was going to marry somebody like Troy, he'd left my mom and me and joined the enemy.

I'd been afraid he would. But at the same time, I never thought he really would. But now I sort of knew it was all over. He was gone. My mom was gone. I was the only one of the three of us left.

Stan was looking at me funny when I happened to notice him again. "Brady? You okay?" He sounded truly concerned, but it was probably a big act.

"Sure," I said. "I can't go out to dinner though. I'm sleeping over at somebody's house tonight. Is that okay?"

"Probably," Stan said. "Whose? Harold's?"

"Nobody you know," I said. "A kid named Gareth."

They wouldn't care, I thought. They weren't like Stan and Troy. They were like Stan and my mom used to be: people who let you sleep over any time you felt like it and just be glad to see you without asking any questions.

"Gareth," Stan said. "Unusual name. I guess it's okay. Leave his phone number." He said it sort of absent-mindedly, though, like he was already thinking of something else, old Troy probably. I didn't bother to tell him there was no phone.

"You'll be home tomorrow morning?"

"Maybe," I said, "unless I go to Alaska."

He laughed. He sounded pretty relieved. He was probably glad to get telling the good news over with. And probably glad to get rid of me for the whole night too, I thought.

"I'm not kidding. I mean it." I said. Without a smile either.

He didn't say anything but I could tell he didn't take me seriously. He was the enemy. He had the power. And he knew it took money to run away. Lots of it. Or else you ended up sitting alone and hungry in some crummy bus station with some maniac trying to take you home so he could dismember you or something.

I cut school that day. I don't do that too often, but what with all the things that happened the night before, I couldn't stand the thought of school; all the yelling and messing around that went on at lunchtime in the cafeteria, having the quiz in algebra and being yelled at by Mr. Purcell in Woodworking I about the tie rack I was making that got uglier every day. Since it was Friday, I thought I'd have the whole weekend to recover. If Stan asked, I'd tell him the reason I cut was I needed to be alone.

I didn't think he'd care. He was usually pretty decent about stuff like that. He usually understood.

It was another foggy morning, cold and damp. The bell on the buoy—a lonesome sound—and the dull boom of the foghorns called to each other like invisible dinosaurs along the coast.

I took a bag of marshmallows, a couple of apples, and a bag of barbecue potato chips with me for Excalibur. I knew he didn't need to eat but I liked giving him stuff he'd never tasted before anyway.

The beach, a dim, mysterious place that smelled like seaweed that morning, and with only the sound of the ocean out there where you couldn't see it, was empty except for me. The dunes had disappeared. There was no wind. It was perfectly still: fog-white and sea-damp wherever I walked. So fog-bound, all I could see was the wet sand in front of my feet. I watched my feet walk over it. It was sort of neat the way the fog got thin enough to see through when I got close to it, but it was still sort of mysterious. It always is.

It felt good to be all by myself on my way to see Excalibur. Monday seemed a long way off and even the good news Stan had told me about the world coming to an end seemed far away for the moment.

What I really wanted to do was take off, just go someplace where I'd never have to see Stan again. Or anybody. If I'd had a choice I would've picked a cabin somewhere away off up a mountain, miles from anybody, to live in all alone. And for food, just pick berries or something. Of course, I realized it was a pretty stupid idea and would never work out or anything.

I thought of selling my comic book collection, which was pretty valuable. I thought I could sell it and just keep the money until Stan and old Troy were married and had me all enrolled in Stoneygate Military Academy ("where boys become teenage sadists"). Or the Applegate Village School for sickos and wackos—and then just take off. I would leave without a word, I thought. And I would never come back.

I felt better after I thought of selling my comic book collection—like I had something to fall back on that belonged to me and could help me escape, like I wasn't so helpless anymore.

I began to feel a lot better in fact. The fog was burning off. By the time I climbed to the top of the Dogs, the day was clear and bright without a cloud in the sky. The sun felt so good on my back. I sat up there on the Dogs for a while, looked out over the ocean that was changing from gray to dark blue, and watched the gulls fish in the water below. It was pretty decent sitting up there like that, taking deep breaths of clean salty air.

Excalibur lifted his armed bronze head when I slid through the crack in the rock. He was lying down so I had no idea how much he'd changed until he stood up, but then how can I tell you how I felt when I really saw him? Part of it was awe, part of it was horror with a lot of something else mixed in.

He'd grown again, but now he was enormous, the size of one of the big dinosaurs, of *Tyrannosaurus rex*. Standing upright, the top of his head was not far from the hole in the vaulted ceiling of the cave. His wings, which lay folded close to his sides, were mighty. I saw the great muscles, bunched and strong as steel, that held them to his shoulders. There was no telling, without seeing, what his wingspread would be. I was certain, though, that the cave was already too small for him to be able to open them out as wide as they could go.

That wasn't all. Everything about him was different from the day before: either larger or sharper or brighter and more clearly defined. The dull gold barbs on his bronze claws were two feet long. The deadly looking scarlet sting on his tail must've been all of five feet. The patterns on his wings were clearer and he shone like a living jewel—not like he had before, but differently, in colors that lived and breathed like the changing fires in his eyes, that blazed from within, the way the colors on fishes' sides surge and flow just before they die. Only Excalibur wasn't dying. He was more vivid and alive than ever. And the beautiful, hideous brute that moved and lived behind the dull gold mask of his face was closer to the surface than ever before. He was magnificent, wonderful, fantastic.

Nobody—unless they were from outer space themselves—had ever seen anything like him. He was a celestial thing; nothing like him had ever come from earth.

When I saw him like that, something happened inside me. I felt like running fast, dancing on water, or yelling with happiness: I went slightly crazy, but *good* crazy, the way you'd feel if you tore through the night sky on a comet or watched a million fireworks go off at once.

But even as I thought how wonderful Excalibur was, at the same time, I saw what a horrible thing was happening. He was beautiful but what I'd been afraid would happen, had happened. He was trapped. The cave was too small. Already he couldn't spread his wings wide enough to fly upward; he was too big to get through the hole in the ceiling anyway, even if he could. Another day of growth like that and he wouldn't be able to move at all.

The cave that had been his nest would be his coffin. He was going to die.

The thought hit me like a blow right between the eyes. It took a while for my mind to stop reacting and be able to hear his answer, which, when it came, was:

That he wouldn't die. Hadn't he told me that before? He was immortal.

But everything dies.

No, nothing really died. Everything in the universe knew that. He knew that when he was still in the egg, even before he was in the egg. Nothing died, things only grew and changed and became more and more themselves forever.

All the same, he'd have to get out of the cave. He couldn't stay there much longer.

When he needed to leave the cave, he would leave the cave.

Yeah, but by then he might not be able to get out. How exactly did he plan to get through solid rock?

If he needed to leave the cave, nothing could stop him. He was not like me. He wasn't confined to any one shape.

But then why had he chosen the shape he had? Why the size, the terrible teeth and claws, the poisonous sting? Did he belong to some species of predator in the place he came from? Or did he need them to protect himself from something that preyed on its own kind in outer space?

There were no predators in outer space. Only earth creatures like myself thought in terms of death and killing.

I still wondered why he'd taken the shape of a large fierce-looking monster that was just the thing to get him destroyed if he ever left the cave. As far as his shape was concerned, he'd told me before that I knew more about that than he did. His present size and shape had been my decision. He lost me there. His thought processes were so different from mine, they confused me. I felt I was sailing somewhere in outer space, among ideas that were like galaxies of stars, but too far away from earth for me to think about myself or anything else I knew about. Or even Excalibur. If he wasn't what he seemed to be, a beautiful monster shut up in a cave, then what was he?

A thought, a tree, a cloud, a wild thing, a monster in a cave, he was nothing and everything and anything I liked.

What he said was always over my head. I wasn't ever able to understand Excalibur, and I guess part of me didn't want to understand, either. It was like flying; I might have been able to if I hadn't been afraid to take my feet off the ground. But I was afraid, so I told myself that understanding wasn't everything either; there were other ways to communicate—so after he told me that, I didn't wonder about anything else. I just took an apple from the bag. I stretched up as tall as I could and held it as high as possible. He bent down and took it.

I did wonder if he liked it.

He liked it but he preferred stones because he liked crunching them up with his teeth.

So I handed him a stone. I was feeling pretty decent again. Even if I couldn't understand Excalibur, even if I wasn't quite convinced of what he told me, still I felt better and a lot less worried about what could happen to him than I was before. He was so sure himself that he would be all right. I almost believed him.

As I said, I started to feel pretty good. I sort of relaxed. I took a couple of rides in Excalibur's claw up to his head to look in his mouth, which was like looking down a mine shaft through a spiked gate like a portcullis, and then back again. I took my sneakers off and dug my toes in the cool wet sand. Then I opened the bag of barbecue potato chips and shared them with Excalibur. And then as usual, he ate the bag. After that, we just sat there together for a while. It was so quiet you could hear the few sounds there were: the hiss and gurgle of the water as it touched the sand, the scream of a gull on the beach outside, and my own breath that came in and out in a little whistle from something in my nose. But Excalibur was perfectly still. I looked up to see if his sides moved in and out, but they didn't.

You're not breathing, I thought.

I don't get my life from air.

Where do you get it from then?

You know. Everything in the universe knows that.

I don't.

But you do. You've just forgotten it for the time being. But sooner or later you'll remember.

It felt just so good to be there with him that I didn't want to argue. I leaned back against the wall of the cave and closed my eyes. As long as I was in the cave with Excalibur, nothing worried me. It was only outside the cave I got afraid.

Excalibur closed his eyes too. He had to stand because he couldn't lie down in the cave anymore. He looked peaceful though. But also like he didn't care much either way, whether I stayed or left. It was dumb, I know, but I felt a little hurt. I even wondered if after all, he really cared whether I came to the cave or not. Or how he would feel if we were separated and he never saw me again. Was he afraid that might happen, the way I was? Or didn't he even care?

He had closed his beautiful eyes, but as I thought those things, he opened them again so that I could see the flames and that mute mysterious thing that always moved behind the mask of smoky gold. It made me catch my breath just to see him.

Goodbye, I thought, until tomorrow.

Until tomorrow.

11
Letting Go

It's a pretty long way from the Dogs to the Andersen house. As I walked it that day, I sort of absentmindedly looked for the glass balls you find on the sand sometimes and thought how I wouldn't be walking there at all if it hadn't been for the good news about Stan and old Troy, and the way I needed to be somewhere else when they were around.

Dinner at Luigi's with my elbow in some stranger's spaghetti because the tables were too close together and to have to sit there while Stan and old Troy gazed into each others' eyes and decided what was going to become of me after the big day seemed pretty horrible. And as far as I could see, life from then on was going to be one long dinner at Luigi's. So I needed a place to go to. I needed to be with people I liked who liked me back.

But another reason I was on my way to see them again was because Gareth seemed like a lonely kid. He was way too young for somebody my age to hang out with or anything, but he'd wanted me to come back so much that even if I hadn't wanted to, I probably would've felt I had to sooner or later.

I saw them as I came to the top of the hill: two little figures down on the dunes. They waved when they saw me and Gareth jumped up and down a few times; you could tell by the way he did it how excited he was. You could forget how excited or disappointed you could be when you're only about five, until you're around somebody like Gareth. I was glad I came that day just for the way it made him jump around.

He started in to talk in his high, excited voice the instant I was able to hear him. He had some stuff on the beach he wanted me to see, he said, some super cool, neat stuff. And he'd seen a deer and could I stay a long time and have dinner with them and did I like hamburgers and could I sleep over, because hamburgers were what they were having for dinner. Mr. Bjornsen delivered a whole load of groceries that day so there were hamburgers and candy and everything and his mom was going to make french fries—not the frozen kind, real ones—and he had a whole coffee can full of fiddler crabs, would I like to see them?

All she said was "Hi," but you could tell she was really glad to see me too. It was neat to be welcome and sort of important and wanted like that. It felt really good— so good it made me realize how long it'd been since I'd felt like that.

Gareth and I went to see the crabs right away. They were in this coffee can he'd set up against the side of this big log on the beach. We stood and looked at all of them in there, crawling all over each other with their pincers waving in the air. We watched how one crab would start on the bottom of the pile and climb up over the backs and faces of the others and step all over them to get to the top only to be pulled down and shoved to the bottom again. The whole thing was sort of depressing. I looked into the can and named one crab Stan and watched to see what happened to him. He stayed on the bottom and let the others step all over him.

After a while I said, "Okay, lets dump 'em out."

He didn't want to though.

"It took me a long time, a year, to get them."

"If you leave them in the can," I said, "they'll start to eat each other."

He looked at them in a disgusted, doubtful way.

"They will?"

I remembered all the coffee cans of crabs I'd collected when I was five.

"They sure will," I said.

So we turned them out and watched them rush away in all directions. There was a sort of regretful look on Gareth's face as he watched them go but he didn't make any move to stop them. When they were gone and only the empty coffee can lay on its side on the sand, he said, "Come on. Now I'll show you something really neat."

As he ran ahead he yelled back over his shoulder, "It's not there, it's on the next beach."

I knew what it was. There was an old beached wreck of a tugboat—the *C. C. Cherry*—on that beach. The year I was ten this girl, Nina, and I played on it all summer long. Nina was a neat girl. She was really smart in school but she was pretty bloodthirsty too. And she was good at thinking up stuff to play. So all summer long two years ago we were Flint and Kidd, Blackbeard and Henry Morgan. We sailed the *C. C. Cherry* through the Dry Tortugas. And on our best days her decks ran with blood.

Sometimes we talked about getting other kids to make up the crew but somehow we never did. I guess we both thought other kids might've spoiled it. We were just right as we were. And so all that summer we played there by ourselves and then she moved to California and I never played on the *C. C. Cherry* again.

I never realized how much I missed those games, though, until that afternoon in June when Gareth, all excited, showed me the boat.

I didn't let on I'd seen her before. Little kids always like to show you stuff and get really upset if you've seen it already or anything.

We came over the crest of a dune and he proudly pointed her out to me, as if he was the only kid in the world who'd ever seen her. I gasped and everything and said, "Wow, a boat! All right!" in this really impressed voice. He looked awfully pleased.

The *C. C. Cherry*. There were rust stains around every nail head in her. She looked smaller and more ready to come apart at the seams than when I'd played on her. Gareth and I walked all around her splintered, slanting deck. He showed me the wheelhouse, the hold, and her name painted on her broad stern, which had once been a chocolate brown and was now a faded tan.

I remembered when Nina and I made broadswords and how on our good days practically nobody had survived. And how we sat on the boat when we'd finished playing with our legs hanging over the side, ate sandwiches we'd brought along, and bragged about ourselves to each other.

But so far as Gareth was concerned, I could see the boat was his own private discovery and most secret treasure. You could tell it was a big compliment that he showed her to me at all.

He didn't know what to do with her though. Once aboard, he just sort of ran wild up and down the deck, in and out of the wheelhouse and cabin. It was pretty clear somebody had to show him what you did with a boat like that. Besides, I thought, as long as he had her to play on, he might as well know how to use her the right way. You don't need anybody else for games like that anyway. You can always make up the crew if you have to.

So right then and there I showed him how to play. We did *Mutiny on the Bounty*. I let him be Captain Bligh. I was Mr. Christian and everybody else. He never did have much of an idea of what the whole thing was about but he knew enough to be Captain Bligh. And you could see right away what a smart little kid he was by the way he followed the action. At the same time it made me feel weird though. Because inside myself I laughed at most of the stuff we did. And that made me feel old, because two years ago it wouldn't have seemed funny to me at all. It would've seemed okay.

We stayed on the boat so long that when we got back to the Andersen house it was supper time. The Andersen front door was wide open. We could smell french fries. The sun was low over the ocean.

The rest of the evening, the rest of the night really, was like a dream. I thought of Stan and old Troy eating their linguine with clams and having a bottle of Chianti but they seemed unreal and far away. But on the other hand, the three of us, as we sat at the kitchen table eating burgers and fries—that were homemade—with the sun pouring its last light into the ocean and the pines on the bluff behind us all black and on guard as if it was night already, didn't seem real either.

"Green pop or red?"

I said green. She smiled at me so I smiled back. I'd given up my weirdness watch about the same time I stopped thinking about all the stories I'd heard about her. I can't say when I stopped believing them any more than I can tell you when I stopped wanting her to be weird and somebody who walked with the dead. By that time, all I knew was I liked her a lot and that anybody could see that whatever she was, it wasn't ordinary. She was somebody. You could tell by a lot of little things she did. Like when she mentioned the soda pop, she said, "It's not the healthy kind," and laughed. She had this nice laugh that sort of sat behind whatever she said and made you want to laugh too. "It's the good old poison kind. You know. Three flavors. Red. Green. Purple."

What I'm trying to say is, there was something neat about the way she knew everybody likes the poison kind of pop with their burgers. Which meant she still remembered what being a kid was like. And why it tasted the best. My mom would've known, too. But somebody like old Troy would've probably served grapefruit juice and frozen fries with her burgers. If she made burgers at all.

And another thing was, we all ate the same stuff. I mean, she didn't go and do something all different and adult, like pour herself a glass of wine while we had pop. She had pop, too.

We ate off paper plates on a bare table. Which was nice because you didn't have to worry like you did at Le Moin's house, where if you spilled something on the tablecloth you felt like you ought to walk out on the terrace and blow your brains out with your service revolver or something.

She didn't treat Gareth like he was nothing but a little kid either. I mean, she was nice to him and all but she didn't treat him like he was dumber than we were or anything. She didn't ask me how I liked school either. In fact, we didn't even talk too much. We just sat there together and peacefully ate our burgers and watched the ocean.

The fries were really good. They made me think of Fat

George's and how Gareth and his mom probably would've liked it there. You could tell they were the kind of people who'd like to eat a Mastodon burger and make their own custom-built sundaes afterward. In my mind I put her and Gareth in one of those big booths they have there with a few Mastodons, a plate of bottomless fries, and a couple of chocolate shakes on the table, with Stan and me on the other side. It looked pretty good to me. So then I told them about Fat George's. She said it sounded good and that she'd like to go there some day. Gareth was all excited about the video games and wanted to go there right away, that instant. The only way I kept him from being really disappointed was by telling him the entire story—scene by scene and word for word—of *The Incredible Shrinking Man*.

We sat outside on the porch while I told it. It wasn't dark yet but it wasn't exactly light either. The sky was getting dark but some pink and purple flowers in the yard looked so bright they were startling. From where we sat the beach looked far away and lonely with the sand all dim and gray like something in an old and faded photograph. Someplace from another time and no place you'd want to be.

They both sat quietly on the top of the porch steps while I told them the story of *The Incredible Shrinking Man*. Which is a film, in case you didn't know, about this guy who gets smaller and smaller by degrees over this period of time. It doesn't have an exactly happy ending either and that's one thing I like about it. I mean, he shrinks up into nothing in the end, like you know he will. But it's not like he's dead or anything either. He sort of goes into infinity and outer space—you see all these stars and a voice says something like how nothing is ever lost in the universe and that everything has a place, no matter how small. I always liked the way it ended. I thought it was cool to end it that way. Even before the accident I liked it. After my mom was gone I liked the part about how everything has a place out there in infinity. It always made me feel better. I mean, for about a split second I felt really happy every time I saw it end that way.

Gareth liked the story a lot. He wanted to see the film, of course, and I almost said he could come to my house and watch it the next time it came on *Chiller Theater*. I almost said it. I knew if I did, he'd be all pleased and excited and everything, but I don't know. I wasn't sure I wanted to get all that mixed up with him. He was such a little kid. But then I felt mean, because they both acted so nice, like neither of them ever thought of my age, or if I were too old or too young for anything concerned with them.

No such idea ever seemed to enter their heads. And they had no TV themselves because the Andersen house had no electricity. It was too far down the beach.

When it got full dark we went inside and lit the kerosene lamp. Gareth watched the flame inside the chimney and rubbed his eyes. He was pale the way little kids get just before they fall asleep. Darkness lay soft in all the corners of the house. The shadows were softer than the ones from electric light. They seemed to go with the silence.

Gareth's mom sat on the ugly Andersen couch. Gareth lay on it full length with his head in her lap. And I sat on an Andersen rocking chair.

"The weather's going to change tonight," she said. "And my guess is, for the worse. Hear the wind? If I were out on the water right now, I'd head for shore."

"My dad has a sailboat," I said. "She's called *Beruthiel*."

She smiled at me. "The queen of the cats," she said.

Gareth was fast asleep. As we talked, she sort of stroked his hair and brushed it off his forehead so that he smiled in his sleep. It looked so nice. He looked so safe and happy it made me lonesome. I wished it was my mom doing that. I wished it was me.

"I love to sail," she said. "I'd get a boat, if we were going to stay here for sure."

"Why can't you stay?"

"I can if I want to," she said. She gave me this look without a smile anywhere in it. "There's nothing to stop me. Nobody's after me. I'm not in any kind of trouble. And, in spite of what they say about me, I'm neither a witch nor a cannibal."

I was just so surprised. I never thought she knew about all the stories. I mean, that just knocked me over, her knowing. I wanted to ask her how she knew, but couldn't think how to do it. Because for some stupid reason I didn't want her to know I'd heard the stuff they said about her. Don't ask me why. Maybe I was just embarrassed. Anyhow, it didn't matter because the next minute she told me anyway.

"I know what they say about me. I hear it all from Chris. He tells me every time there's a new story. And that's every time he brings out a load of groceries."

I thought of Cousin Chris with his big flat face, flounder eyes, and the reputation he had for being as close-mouthed as he was closefisted. I wondered if she had any idea of how much he must've liked her to have gone out of his way to tell her what he did.

"He's a nice man," she said.

"He's okay," I said sort of doubtfully, because I knew him better than she did.

"He's nice," she said. "But I can't say the same for what you might call the local imagination. It is definitely not nice."

I shook my head. No, it wasn't. Not at all.

"I wonder why people always think the worst when they don't know anything about you," she said. She seemed sort of sad. "Why couldn't they have just thought I might be somebody who wanted to be alone? Why couldn't they have just thought I was harmless and nice when I came here? Why did they have to think I was crazy and strange and mean?"

I thought about the burlap sack and the horned man. I shook my head to show I was listening and knew what she meant but hadn't much to say about it. It was embarrassing in a way, because of course I'd believed all that stuff about her too. Or wanted to, anyway.

She looked down at Gareth and frowned. "Anyway, why should I have to explain to all those people why I don't come to their general store?"

So there, once and for all, went the walking dead and forbidden knowledge and all the rest. Just like that. Just blown away and gone in about two minutes. All that was left was Gareth's mom. I can't say it came as a big surprise or anything by that time. But all the same, it really messed me up. Because of course, it was my last big, final hope that just exploded in my face. I made one frantic grab after it. I was too horribly disappointed to do anything else. And anyway, I still secretly hoped that maybe I was wrong about her, that late as it was, she might still be something she wasn't. Or if not, then she might change so that she could say she knew where what I looked for was and how to get there. That's how weird I was by that time. So before I even had a chance to think or knew I was going to say anything at all, I heard myself ask her, loud and clear, with no warning whatsoever, if she thought dead people went anywhere after they died.

It was a dumb, weird thing to ask just then. And after I'd said it the words hung in the air between us and we stared at each other oddly for an instant.

"What?" she said.

I didn't exactly want to repeat it but I did.

"I said, do you think people go anyplace after they die?"

"What do you mean, anyplace? You mean like heaven?"

"No, not there." I thought of the big huge waiting room with George Washington and Moses and John Lennon all sitting there.

"I meant," and it was like danger to say it, like falling through space, like the jump off the Needle when I finally got the words out of my mind into the air. "I meant, do you think there might be some other place, not heaven, that they might go to? When they leave here?"

She looked at me in a kind of baffled way, and said, "Like where?"

"I thought there might be a line," I said. "Somewhere. Some line between life and death that you might be able to step over, to get there." I think I gave her a pretty hopeful look about there. "And that there might be this place you could even go to and get them out of some way?"

"I wish was there was," she said. Her eyes were soft and green as ferns as she thought about it. "If there was, if I knew there was a line like that," her eyes were bright as lanterns, "I'd never stop looking until I found it. I'd walk to the end of the world if I had to."

"So would I," I said. "I would too."

"And when I found it," she said, "I'd step right over it and take him by the hand and lead him back."

"And then what?" I was all excited somehow, though I wasn't sure why.

"And then," she said, "we'd pretend he never went away. That there'd never been an accident."

When she said that word—accident—something happened to my insides the way it always did. I didn't want to ask, I didn't even want to hear about it but she told me anyway.

"He was killed in Central America last year—Gareth's father—by guerillas. He was a journalist. He was shot. They said it was an accident. That's why I'm here, if you want to know. I came here because I needed to be some-place where we'd never, ever been together. Where I could be alone to think and try to, try to—"

"My mom was killed in a car crash a year ago," I said. I never told anybody about the accident because it was almost impossible to speak the words out loud. But I said them to her. And when I said them I felt like she looked—that is, ready to cry.

She didn't say she was sorry to hear it or anything. She didn't have to because after I said it she looked at me and her eyes said everything she needed to say better than words ever could, in fact, that look of hers was a lot like my mom's smile: something valuable, something you'd want to keep.

Neither of us said anything for a while after that. Then, because I had to know, I broke our silence by saying, "You think there is?"

"Think there's what?"

"Someplace. A land of the dead. Or something."

She didn't answer right away. You could tell she was thinking about what I said. Then (and I almost closed my eyes and stuck my hands over my ears the way Gareth did when he was afraid to hear the answer) she said, "Yes, I think there is. I don't *know* for sure. But I think they do go on. They don't just stop being. What a waste that would be! But if there is a place—another place where they're supposed to be—it must be where they belong, I mean. I don't think any mistakes are ever made on that level."

"But—"

"The real mistake would be to try to hang on to them," she said, "because, who knows? It might hold them back some way and not let them be free enough to go on the way they're meant to. Anyway, that's what I think. And that's what I'm doing. Every day that I live here and walk along the shore, I'm letting go."

I thought of my mom.

"It's pretty hard to do," I said. "Isn't it?"

"Yes. It's pretty hard to do."

Gareth woke up and said he dreamed he ate a ham sandwich and could he have one? Nobody said how late it was or that he ought to go back to sleep or anything. We all just went to the kitchen. I couldn't eat anything myself. I was still pretty disappointed. But I watched the others pull stuff from the refrigerator (which ran on kerosene, in case you're wondering) and make sandwiches for themselves. Then we all went outside onto the Andersen front porch so we could watch the sky while they ate.

The wind was high out there, but not cold, just fresh. Far away across the dunes you could just barely hear the steady roar of the water: a solid sound that never stopped, that went on forever. Tall white clouds with bright silver edges made towers in the sky. And the full moon, all sharp edged and fresh cut, made a perfect port-hole that opened into brightness, so that everyone could see that heaven is not gold but silver. And that was when, and where, I left my mom. In all that light, out there. I let her go—to space and stars and brightness, where she belonged.

12
Storm

The next day, Saturday, was one of the weirdest days of my life. To begin with, the weather had changed during the night and was like something out of a horror comic. It was so hot, I woke up sweating, with a fly buzzing in my ear.

I was still in a dream, so I didn't know where I was at first. I thought I was home and that my mom was there. Then I opened my eyes and there was this fly—one of the fat, soft kind called bluebottles, crawling on my cheek. There were a lot of them buzzing and thumping against the window screen. There was a hole in the screen and that was how my fly got in. When I got up and walked over to the hole I saw why they were like that. There was no wind. It was an ugly day: a still, white sky full of hot, heavy air, the kind of weather that pushed flies against window screens and indoors, into people's food and faces—the kind of day that promised to be bad from start to finish. With a threat behind it all that made you feel that something even worse for everybody might be in the works.

Gareth had slept in his mom's room, but he came in when he heard me get up. He'd been up a long time, he said. He'd found a dead gull on the beach already, and did I have to go home right away or could we have a funeral first? He handed me a banana, which I ate. Then we went straight to the beach.

The day was so strange. The tide was out and the ocean dark gray and hardly moving, thought I knew it still hissed and muttered to itself out there, like a gigantic beast, all chained up and planning to break out. The air felt like damp cotton and was full of midges and other flying things that bit our arms and dived in our ears and noses as we walked. And the beach was ugly that morning, littered with all kinds of junk: plastic bottles and rubber boots, dead birds and fish left by the tide, so that it looked like a garbage heap and stank of rotten seaweed.

We passed formations of gulls that stood on the sand all facing in the same direction and not moving—like an army without generals that just stood there and waited for a war or some other big event.

Big black crows wheeled in the dead air in rude and noisy circles, jeering at the gulls and anything else that had to obey the rules. And as I watched them, my own troubles came wheeling back into my head, as big and black as crows.

We found Gareth's gull. It had been dead a pretty long time, but looked lively all the same, because it was full of hopping sand fleas. Gareth felt sorry for it, he said. So we buried it above the waterline. I scooped a hole in the sand. Gareth had brought along a box. You could tell he'd had bird funerals before. I was pretty experienced at that kind of funeral myself. And that was why, when I saw the bright scarf he pulled from his pocket, I said, "Are you sure it's okay to use that?"

Because I used to take my mom's stuff sometimes for things like funerals and had been in big trouble for doing it, in my time. But I guess Gareth was smarter, because he said he was sure and showed me where the big hole in the scarf was.

So we wrapped the body in the scarf, stuck it in its coffin, and buried it. Then we made a headstone and stuck it at the head of the grave.

"Say a prayer," Gareth said.

"Okay," I said. "Ashes to ashes and dust to dust." That was what *we* always said, the kids on the beach, whenever we buried anything. Gareth opened his eyes, which he'd shut so tight they'd screwed up, and smiled. He looked at me with his big clear eyes.

"That's okay," he said. Who knew what he meant by that?

She'd fixed breakfast when we got back. It was pancakes with maple syrup. We ate them at the table in the kitchen. And as we ate she kept looking out the window.

"Look at that sky," she said finally. "Feel all the electricity in the air? And the birds are flying inland—there's going to be a storm. I think it might be going to be a big one." She sort of shivered. "Can't you feel how everything's waiting for something to happen?"

"Will you be okay out here?"

"The water can't come up this far," she said. "Even if

there was a tidal wave. So, we'll be all right. And the dunes shelter us from the wind. But you'd better stay until it's over."

"I can't," I said. I thought about Excalibur in his cave. "There's something I have to see about."

She was like my own mom; she never bothered with a lot of silly questions. So when I said that, all she said was, "Then you'd better go. There's no telling when the storm might hit the coast."

I knew she was right so we said good-bye. I promised Gareth the next time *The Incredible Shrinking Man* came on TV he could sleep over at my house and watch it.

A sheet of green light ripped the clouds apart and flared across the horizon. There was the sound of thunder far away over the water. A sudden rush of wind brought with it a few big drops of rain.

"It's coming closer," she said. "You'd better go."

After I came down from the bluff I headed for the Dogs. I knew Excalibur would be safe in the cave even if it was wet, but I wanted to see him anyway. He'd never seen a storm. I thought if I wasn't there to explain what was happening he might be terrified, might even stampede or something (which only shows how little I knew about him even then), and hurt himself.

By the time I'd climbed over the Dogs the sky was almost black as night, though after that first gust of wind, no rain had fallen after all. And the wind was gone too; the air was still, as if it were inside a room.

You could feel how everything was just sitting there

waiting, being saved up for the main event. It made you nervous, that feeling of something big just on the edge of being about to happen; like some huge animal ready to pounce and tear up the beach with everything on it. I wondered how I could get over the Dogs and back down the beach if it broke while I was still in the cave. All the same, I wanted, I had to see Excalibur no matter what, so I kept going.

The sun came out for one instant as I came into the cave. It made him shine all green and gold in such a blaze of light he almost hurt my eyes. Then the sun went in again and in that more sober light, I could see him better. Much better, clear enough to see the truth—which was that the process was complete. Excalibur was fully gown, entirely evolved, and couldn't be more powerful or more beautiful than he already was.

At the same time I saw that, I knew, I absolutely knew without reasoning it out at all, that he was also free of the cave. That the thing was out of our hands, Excalibur's and mine, that it had been decided without us that it was time for him to leave. And that even though he was still there for me to see and close enough to touch, everything was finished and this was the last time we would ever be together in the cave.

I stood there and just looked at him. I tried to tell myself how lucky I'd been to find him at all; how I'd been the only one to see him come out of the egg, the only one to know he was there. But it didn't work. All I really felt was, this was the end. I would never see him again. There would be no more going to the cave, no more thinking about being able to see him later when I was away from him. I would be more alone than ever because he'd been there and was gone. It was over. I knew it had to happen sooner or later, but I guess I never felt worse about anything in my life—not even when they told me about my mom. And I couldn't tell him how I felt. I loved him too much. Not the way you love girls or your family, which is usually half phony and half sad anyway. I mean I loved him in a clear way, like you love birds flying over the sea on a windy day or a night full of falling stars. And he was sort of too beautiful as he stood there, all proud and shining, like a super beast from somewhere wonderful not on this earth, to be spoiled by grief or anything. I didn't want to touch him or tell him good-bye or anything. I just waned him to know how I felt about him.

He did, too. He bent his head to look straight at me with his fiery eyes and as we looked at each other, the brute, hideously beautiful, beautifully hideous, that always moved behind his golden mask came closer to the surface than it had ever come before. For one instant I almost saw, and the seeing was like falling through outer space past billions of stars, a hundred thousand miles a minute.

I shut my eyes. I looked away and fell down to earth. The walls of the cave were solid around Excalibur and me again, the rocks and the mini-beach were still there. I wondered though, for how long. I wondered what would become of him once he was out of the cave. Where would he go?

He would go where he was meant to go.

What would he do?

Whatever he was supposed to do.

But what if he were to meet something terrible out there? What if something terrible happened to him once he left the cave? Horrible things happened all the time, every minute of the day, out there.

Nothing horrible could happen to him. It wasn't possible. How many times did he have to tell me he lived by laws I didn't understand?

But the storm—flying through the storm—there was a storm coming.

What was a storm?

A storm was a terrible thing, with tidal waves and winds that could tear up the earth, drown houses, and kill you. He ought to wait until the storm was over before he left the cave—however he planned to do that.

If that was all a storm was, I was not to worry. Storms couldn't touch what he was made of. Material objects were all they could destroy. But if they could destroy creatures like myself, the sooner I left the cave, the better, if one were coming. Otherwise I might be hurt.

I couldn't leave, though. Not just yet. I was too miserable thinking I would never see him anymore.

But hadn't he already told me that once I was able to see him at all, I could never really loose him ever again?

But I wouldn't see him again like this.

I would see him again, though. He would always be there to help me if I needed help. But sometimes not in the shape or way I expected. I would have to keep my inner eye open or I might not recognize him when I saw him.

I wanted to understand what he told me but it was too difficult, as usual. I thought a certain way because I was human and Excalibur thought another way because he was . . . what was he? He never really ever told me.

He was what he was. What was there before me and what would be there after me.

But, so I would know what he said was true and so I wouldn't be able to fool myself into thinking he was just imaginary, some kind of fantasy perhaps, he would give me something to keep with me forever.

He turned his shining head and pulled a scale from his shoulder with his teeth, as delicately as if it were a feather, and dropped it into my hand. It felt cool and burning at the same time as it blazed in my palm with a green fire. We watched it melt and dissolve away until nothing was left but a tiny gold-green smear on my skin and a tingling feeling in my hand.

You'll have that on your hand forever as a sign I'm here. And now, good-bye.

Good-bye. Good-bye, Excalibur the Beautiful.

The storm broke just as I climbed down off the Dogs and onto the beach. There was a streak of lightning, a crack of thunder, a roar of wind, and then the whole world went wild. A wall of wind and water hit me full in the face and pushed against me so hard that I could barely walk. I was blinded and wet through in about two minutes. The wind kept on attacking me and nearly pushed me over. The sound it made was like about a thousand maniacs yelling as loud as they could in my ears. I couldn't see where I was and I could hardly even see where I was going, so at first I couldn't think of anything but just bracing myself against the wind and putting one foot ahead of the other.

I was lost. There were landmarks but I couldn't see them, so I didn't even know if I was going in the right direction down the beach. You couldn't see the ocean. You could just hear it, like a ferocious beast that was out there tearing things to pieces. I kept expecting to feel seawater over my ankles any minute; and knew that if that happened, I was done for. The sea would be faster than I was. There was nothing to do but keep on walking, though, until I could find some sort of shelter somewhere. So that's what I did. But I never expected to make it home. Or to anyplace else. I really thought I'd had it.

The weird thing was, the weather didn't get any better, the way I thought it might. It got worse. With all that water in the air it even got hard to breathe. I began to think I might drown just waking down the beach. And stuff was blowing around, too. I kept getting hit by sand and small flying objects, and if I could've found the woods I would've risked getting my brains knocked out by flying branches just to get out of the wind. And all the time as I stumbled along on the wet sand, I could hear the thunder pounding away up there in the sky and see the forked lightning crash through the rain.

My feet got into deeper sand finally and I knew I was

in the dunes, though I couldn't see them. Then, after what seemed forever, I bumped into a tree and I knew I'd stumbled in the right direction by accident, or luck, or whatever. The ground felt different. I was off the beach and at the edge of the woods.

That day, though, they were not like the woods I knew. The trees were screaming like they were being hurt, twisting and tossing in unbearable pain. I was heading for the underbrush when, just like someone had thrown it at me, a branch hit me hard across the shoulders and knocked me to the ground. I thought my back was broken. I just lay there with the rain pouring down on me and felt like none of my life had really happened: that I'd always just been where I was, on the ground. Every time I breathed it felt like one of those big snakes they have in the Amazon was squeezing me to death.

I don't know how long I lay like that. I only know that when I could move again, I did. I crawled under a bush and stayed there. It was wet and miserable but it was shelter of some kind, and after a while the pain sort of went away. I don't know how long I stayed under the bush either. I thought a lot of stuff, though, while I was there that I won't bore you with, except for this one funny thing: I kept thinking there wasn't any world out there beyond the bush I was under. And no time. There was just the storm and me.

The end of it finally began to come though. The thunder and lightning stopped. Then the wind came down from being a gale to just a stiff breeze and though the rain still poured, the downfall wasn't as heavy anymore. And that was when I came out from under my bush.

It was fully dark by then but since I wasn't being blinded by water anymore, I could see a little. I could tell where the dunes began and once I got back to them I knew which way to walk and where I was—a long way from home but headed in the right direction anyway.

It sure was cold. I guess I was so busy surviving up to then, I hadn't noticed it; but afterward, on the way home, as I walked down the beach with the wind blowing on my wet clothes, I started to shiver like crazy. My teeth were rattling, even my elbows were going. I remembered I hadn't eaten since morning. I hadn't thought about it before, but when I did, it reminded me that I was also cold and wet and really, really tired. I was thinking so hard, in fact, about how uncomfortable I was that I passed an odd-looking object all covered with sand without reacting to it at all. Until it cried, that is. It cried just once, something between a cry and a whimper, but it was loud enough for me to hear, so I stopped.

You should have seen it the way I did when I first bent down to look at it. You would never have known it was a puppy—or anything alive—except that it breathed and you could feel its sides move in and out when you touched it. It was the most miserable object I'd ever seen in my life. Soaking wet, covered all over with sand, with sand in its nose, mouth, and eyes; I didn't think it had a chance. It was too waterlogged. It had been in the storm too long.

But it was still alive so I brushed as much of the sand as I could out of its face and pushed it under my shirt and against my chest to keep it warm. It was shivering even worse than I was. I felt it shuddering away against my chest all the way home.

13
Keeper

She was no beauty. I mean, when I got her back home and looked at her in the light, I saw that in the first place none of her matched. She looked like she'd been made out of leftover parts of other dogs, all sort of thrown together some way, so they wouldn't be wasted.

She had a long body that sat on short stumpy legs. Her head was beagle-sized, with a face that couldn't decide whether to be a coyote or a jackal, so had tried a little of both—though she sort of favored a spaniel around the ears. Not even her eyes were pretty: they were small and light yellow, like a hound's. Her fur was your basic short white with the kind of brown markings that looked more like an accident of nature than anything else. In fact, the only part of her that didn't look accidental was her tail. That looked deliberate—like a mean joke. Her tail was . . . well, in the first place, it was plumed. And it was so outsized it didn't look like it belonged to her at all. When you saw it, you got the feeling she'd lost her own tail someplace and had hurriedly borrowed another from a full-grown setter. It was the sort of tail the nicest person in the world might bend over double with laughing at the sight of it. And dogs are funny: they feel stuff like that. Looking at that tail, I knew it was going to humiliate her all her life. And that even if the rest of her had been better looking, that tail would've taken away any claim to class she might have had. And if about now you're imagining her as one of those cute mutts they feature in Disney films—don't. This pup wasn't cute at all. Visually, she was a disaster.

She was tough, though. Even if she was shivering almost hard enough to shake the flesh off her bones, when I got her home she was still alive, and as far as I could tell, not even sick. I dried her with a towel and washed the sand out of her eyes, nose, and mouth. Then I wrapped her up again, with a hot water bottle, in a blanket I found inside a plastic cover at one end of the sofa. By the time I'd taken off my own wet clothes and put on dry ones she'd stopped shivering and her eyes were open.

The clock said it was only an hour to midnight. By some miracle the electric lines hadn't gone down in the storm. All the lights in our house were on and everything looked normal, except nobody was there. It felt wonderful to be home though, where it was all warm and light, with a refrigerator full of food, after what I'd been through.

I heated some milk for the pup and put her beside the bowl, but she just sprawled on the linoleum, all limp and looking like somebody's worn-out stuffed animal. She was just too tired and scared to eat. I had to dip my finger in the bowl and stick it in her mouth a few times before she'd even start licking it off my finger. But she was smart; it didn't take long before she found out the milk was in the bowl and got more interested. She sniffed at it and then, as she began to lap the milk, she got more and more eager and finally didn't quit until it was all gone. After that I knew she would be okay. I wrapped her in the blanket and put her back on the sofa. She went to sleep right away.

I watched her fall asleep and wondered what a half-grown pup like that was doing out on the dunes. I thought she might've been dumped out of a car, just left there. It's hard to believe anybody would do a thing like that, but people do. It happens at the beach all the time. Or maybe she'd run away from home and got lost trying to find her way back when the storm broke. If that was it, I thought, it was bad luck for her. Because a dog that looked like she did would have trouble finding another. Most people want dogs that are pretty or at least cute. I felt bad for her, knowing she was going to have as hard a life later as she'd probably had already.

I was ravenous by the time I'd taken care of her, though, so I made myself a sandwich—my favorite one, not counting the Mastodon at Fat George's. What I did was get these beans—not the tomato kind, but the molasses kind in a jar—and some white bread and mayonnaise, and made myself three big, slippery, delicious sandwiches with a generous portion of barbecue potato chips and a glass of milk on the side. Then I turned on

Chiller Theater while I ate them and waited for Stan to come home.

It wasn't any good that night, though. It was one of those oldies: the kind with a bad sound track and too much background music and everybody wearing evening clothes. With one of those really dumb, annoying girls in it, the kind who never stays upstairs in her room even if somebody's been murdered already but always has to go wandering around some big house getting other people in trouble trying to save her. And not a monster in the whole film, just a boring insane killer with a mustache and dinner jacket. I kept it on but I didn't watch it. I took another look at the dog instead.

She was dead asleep, breathing hard, and twitching a little. She barked once under her breath and her feet made running motions under the blanket. I wondered if she was having a good or bad dream. Was she still running from the storm? Looking at her like that, for the first time in hours, I thought of Excalibur: so perfect, so proud, so gone. And in that instant, I knew that even if she wasn't beautiful, that dog sleeping in the blanket was my dog from then on and that I was going to keep her for better or for worse. And not because if I didn't take care of her nobody would, or because I felt sorry for her and bad about her tail, either. But because I thought she was tough and probably smart, and I liked her.

Since that was the way it was going to be, I tried to think of a name for her, but nothing came to mind. All I could think of were mean ones that called attention to her looks like "Beauty" or "Wags." I thought of calling her "Troy." Boy, would old Troy have had a fit. I was thinking about how mad she'd be and sort of grinning about it when Stan came in.

I should have said, "burst in," only that sounds too melodramatic. He did though. He came through the back door, which meant he'd been out on the beach. And when I saw the look on his face I began to realize a lot of things I hadn't thought about even once all the time I'd been away from home. Like how it must've looked to Stan that day. I mean, here's your kid, sleeps over at another kid's house and starts home the next morning; but he never gets home and there's a storm. You wait all day to hear from him or about him and finally you go out looking for him, probably thinking all kinds of stuff, like he's been drowned or something. Seeing his face when he came in, I thought he must've really suffered. Like I did, when I worried about Excalibur. Or maybe even worse, how did I know? And there I'd been, not thinking about Stan or his feelings even once that day. Maybe because Stan had been with old Troy so much, taking her places and fighting with her and making plans to get married, I thought he didn't care about me anymore. I don't know.

Anyway, there were no two ways about how Stan felt about me that night. I mean, there I was, sitting there as full of bean sandwiches as a boa constrictor is full of a fawn, with my TV program on and my new dog; and there was Stan, not even speaking when he saw me: just giving a sort of wordless yell and running across the room to grab me in his arms like a crazy man, laughing with relief. He was really glad to see me, no doubt about it. And he didn't get mad once the relief was over, the way most people would have. I just explained (without mentioning Excalibur) that when the storm broke I'd been on the beach, so that I'd had to find shelter and wait it out. Then he explained how he'd gone out to look for me. Nobody was mad at anybody. He noticed the blanket, though, and asked what was in it. I said it was my dog.

"In Troy's new American Heirloom blanket?" Stan asked.

I looked at the blanket—I mean really looked—for the first time and saw that, sure enough, it was fancy and white and one I hadn't seen before.

"She'll kill me," I said.

"Slowly and painfully," Stan agreed. But he looked more interested in the first thing I'd said.

"A dog, you say?"

"My new dog," I said. "I found her on the dunes, coming back just now. She was half dead, but she's okay now."

"A dog," Stan repeated, pleased. He likes animals. I knew in advance he'd never say no to this one. "Let's have a look."

He walked over to the couch and pulled one corner of the blanket away from my pup. He looked at her.

"Oh no," he said, and sort of laughed. When he sort of laughed like that I felt like rushing up and making all kinds of excuses for her and hoped she hadn't understood what the tone of his voice meant or who he was laughing at. And knew this would be the first of hundreds of times I would feel that way.

"I can keep her, can't I?" I said, because it's best to have those things clearly understood from the beginning.

"You'd better keep her," Stan said agreeably. "I don't think anybody else would want her. What are you going to name her?"

"I'll think of something," I said.

We didn't talk much longer after that. We were both tired. When I went to bed I took my dog upstairs with me and that's one thing you can say for guys living together. Stan didn't make a fuss about fleas or getting the sheets dirty or anything. He didn't say a word about it when we said good night.

She slept curled up against my chest as if that was the way she'd always slept. When I put her under the covers she got as close to me as she could, heaved one big sigh, and was fast asleep. Except for once around one o'clock, when she drank some warm milk, and once around four o'clock, when we had our earthquake, we both slept straight through till morning.

14
Trouble

Our earthquake is pretty famous. I forget what it measured on the Richter scale, but it was quite a lot, and it got on national television and everything. A tidal wave went with it and cottages right on the beach disappeared. Nobody was in them but it was still pretty bad.

At the time it happened, before I could think about what it was or be scared or anything, it was over. I mean, I woke up in the middle of the night and got up. Then the floor started to move under my feet. Only I thought there was something wrong with me, not it. Then I saw a little crack break out on the wall and run down it like a fast little vine that branched out into more little cracks. And then it was over.

By morning there was nothing left of the storm either, except that the ocean was rougher than usual and the beach was covered with wreckage. I didn't leave the house right away, though. Stan and I had breakfast together first, for a change, and then we washed my dog. When she was all clean and dry, Stan looked at her.

"On second thought, maybe we should have left the

sand on her," he said. "She looked better that way. Thought of a name yet?"

"Not yet," I said. She'd come over and was fussing around me, wagging her tail.

"Don't laugh," I warned Stan. I could tell by his face he was about to.

"How about 'La Verne'?" he said, "La Verne's a good name."

"I'll think about it," I said.

"Going out to beachcomb? Beachcombing ought to be terrific today."

"Why? Is Troy coming over or something?"

Stan smiled self-consciously.

"Okay," I said, "I'll see you later."

The beach was pretty good that morning. It was a mess, with lots of dead things on it like birds, fish, rats, and rabbits. There was lots of good stuff too, like packing crates, nets, pieces of boats. Everybody was out that day, partly to pick up stuff and partly to see what the storm had done.

What it had done was change the landscape. For one thing, the dunes were different. For another, and this was the big thing everybody wanted to see, the Dogs were gone. They had been literally torn apart, pulled right down, and scattered all over the beach, with everything about them changed. The caves that had been there forever were gone. Just like that.

They were off-limits, at least temporarily. The ranger had put up DANGER KEEP OUT signs all over that part of the beach. But I went there anyway. I knew he would be gone. But I had to know for certain.

There was no trace of him. No trace of anything. The rocks I'd climbed over were gone—at least the way they'd been piled up was gone, and the cave with the white sand mini-beach was gone, like it had never been. It made me feel so weird, seeing all that, that I guess it took something like seeing the Dogs tossed all over the beach like fallen giants, a big thing like that, to make it sink in that Excalibur was really gone.

I felt good about him, in a sad way. I knew he'd be happier where he belonged and that was where I hoped he was: out there in the universe, among the stars. But I missed him. I needed to go on seeing him and knowing he was there. Then I remembered how he'd said once I had seen him I could never be without him again. I opened my hand and looked down at the palm. The tiny gold green mark he'd left me was still there.

Old Troy was at my house when I got back that day. And gloomy Sunday was as thick in the air of our kitchen as the leaves of Sunday paper that lay all over our floor. Stan and his ghoul fiend sat at our kitchen table with coffee cups in front of them. The room was full of silence but the air was heavy with unsaid words. You could almost hear them buzzing angrily like flies if you came into the room suddenly, like I did.

Old Troy stared out the window. Her lips were so small and tight she looked practically mouthless. Stan looked the way he had pretty often lately: depressed, confused, and with a general look of how-did-I-get-into-this on his face.

I just stood there a minute. I didn't know what to do. Old Troy gave me a look that should've been shot out of a blowgun but didn't notice me otherwise. Stan sort of looked at me but that was all. It was pretty obvious I'd stepped into the middle of another big argument. But I couldn't just leave again without saying anything. And I couldn't think of anything to say except that I was back, which would've sounded pretty stupid.

There I was—in plain sight and everything—so, as usual, I said the wrong thing. When I said it, I didn't mean to mess up anything. I was just trying to act at ease and lighten things up a little. I looked at Stan and tried the old Laurel and Hardy routine.

"Call me a taxi." I said. I was glad when his face relaxed for an instant and a Stan Laurel look came into his eyes.

"You're a taxi," Stan never could resist Laurel and Hardy no matter what was going on.

But it didn't last long, because old Troy said, as if she were going on with the same old argument they'd been having before, "I was under the impression you'd promised."

"I only said I'd think about it," Stan said. "And only if everybody agreed."

"It's not up to 'everybody,'" old Troy said with a nasty glance in my direction. "It's up to you and me."

"But how could you just go ahead and do it?" Stan

asked. "That's what I don't understand. It was a very strange thing to do."

"I'm not strange," Troy said.

"But *that* was strange, just doing it and not telling me," Stan said.

"Well," old Troy said, "it's done. And he's going."

"Now just a—ah, let's drop it for now," Stan said. And there was a sort of nasty gleam in his eye, too, when he said it, a look I'd never seen before.

"There's nothing wrong with making arrangements," old Troy said. "It doesn't happen to be a crime."

I knew what they were talking about of course. It was me and how to get rid of me without Stan having to feel too guilty about it. It was just another thing he was leaving up to her to do, like finding his lost keys or making out his income tax. I wondered how she'd do it, old Troy. She was pretty smart, so I thought she'd manage it one way or another. And by that time, in a way, I didn't care. Who wanted to live with old Troy and her cat anyway?

I looked at the tiny green mark on my hand, secretly, so they wouldn't notice. It was still there: Excalibur's promise that everything was really all right even when it didn't seem to be.

I thought a lot of stuff, but all I said out loud was, "Where's my dog?"

She'd heard my voice and was already walking across the floor as fast as she could on her stumpy legs, wagging her awful tail as hard as she could, and making a whole party for herself just because I was home. When she was close, she smiled at me and danced around in dumpy little circles to show how happy she was to see me and how she was my dog, all right.

It made me feel so good the way she licked my hands and tried to kiss my face that I didn't care how gloomy the rest of the kitchen was. But the way things were, I thought it wouldn't hurt anything if old Troy got to like my dog. I didn't dare ask what she thought of her, but I did sort of look in her direction when I said, "I can't think of a name for her."

That was all old Troy needed though. She smiled and said, "How about Quasimodo?"

"Aw, come on," Stan said. He reached down and patted my dog on her head.

Old Troy laughed, unpleasantly. "She's just about the ugliest animal I've ever seen."

"She's a strong little dog," Stan said. You could tell he was trying to be okay to everybody and keep the peace.

"So was the Hound of the Baskervilles," old Troy said. And laughed as if she thought she was being pretty witty about the whole thing all right.

My face got all hot. I wanted to tell her my dog's behind was a hundred times better than her face, but I controlled myself. I couldn't afford to be in the wrong just then or have either of them mad at me.

"I gather you don't entirely approve of her then?" Stan said. He sounded pretty formal and snotty and everything when he said it.

"Am I required to?" She sounded snotty, too.

"Maybe," Stan said. But he stopped being snotty for a second and said pretty nicely, "Aw come on, Troy, knock it off. Don't be such a—what do you really think of the dog?"

I guess since old Troy was already in a bad mood, she thought this was her opening. She didn't waste it either. She looked at my dog the way you'd look at a dirty old piece of something you'd just scraped off the bottom of your shoe. Then she looked at me.

"What do I think of her? I think she's the ugliest dog I've ever seen. I think she should have been drowned at birth. That's what I think of her."

I didn't look at either of them when she said that. I put my face down so my dog could lick my nose. I told myself I didn't care what old Troy thought about my dog. Or about me. Or about anything. I kept quiet, though, because if you went with the feeling in the room, things were bad enough already. But all the same I thought old Troy better not say anything more about my dog.

"I still think you ought to call her La Verne," Stan the Rat said, sort of hurriedly, still in there trying to make things better.

"That's a stupid name," I said. I patted my dog's head. I was getting madder by the minute. She licked my hand. I thought nobody better make anymore fun of her while I was around, or else.

"You really shouldn't name her anything," old Troy said. "It will only confuse her. The people who adopt her are the ones who should name her."

"What do you mean, adopt her?" I sort of yelled. I jumped to my feet. I was really upset by that time. "What are you talking about, adopt her? What people?"

"She'll need a home," old Troy said calmly. She didn't look at me. "So she'll have to go to the pound. That's how homeless animals get homes, isn't it?"

"Hey, Troy," Stan said.

"The *pound!*" I shouted. I was sort of shouting the whole time, by then, because I didn't know what was going on. I was getting really scared. And it was either cry in front of everybody or get mad, so I got mad. "What are you talking about? I wouldn't take her to any pound. Nobody would want her. They'd kill her there."

"Not necessarily," old Troy said, not even trying to sound as if she cared if they did or not.

I gave Stan a furious you'd-better-explain-this look, but didn't speak because my voice sort of broke on the last word of the last thing I said and made me sound as if I were about to cry or something.

Old Troy gave Stan a look at the same time, a warning one. And Stan looked more miserable all the time.

"The thing is, Brady," he said, "the thing is—well, you know how Ivan hates dogs. And when Troy moves in here with Ivan, after we're married, well—having a dog just wouldn't work. I'm as sorry as I can be I didn't think it out better before I said you could keep her. I mean that. But you can see how it would be impossible. You can see that, can't you?"

Ivan the Terrible, old Troy's awful cat. The meanest,

most arrogant, obnoxious animal I've ever known. Even old Troy only liked him because he was so valuable. She always told everybody how few Russian blues there were in the United States. Knowing Ivan, I could see why.

Anyway, after Stan said that to me, I was speechless. And outraged. I thought of lots of things to say, all insulting and rude, but short of blowing Ivan away somehow, there was nothing I could do. That was the trouble. Old Troy had me there. She was always a little ahead of me anyway, when it came to getting whatever she wanted over my dead body. And I knew she always would be.

I stood there and wished my mom was back so I could ask her what to do. Or that Excalibur was still in his cave, so I could run away from them all and go there. Or that I had a friend I could trust besides Le Moin, who wasn't a free agent either, because he was a kid like me.

Then, just as I thought all that, there was a tingling in my hand, urgent as a bell ringing, that was like a telephone call to my mind, and I thought: Gareth's mom.

I was pretty sure she'd help me any way she could, if I needed help. And out there on the dunes, so far away from everybody, a dog would be a good thing to have.

"I'm really sorry, Brady," Stan said. I could tell he really was sorry, too.

"That's okay," I said, cold as ice. I got as much dignified contempt on my face as I could when I said it. "Forget it. I'll give her up if I have to. But she's not going to any pound. I happen to have a friend who'll be glad to take her."

Old Troy laughed.

"I doubt that," she said. She was pretty stupid about some things, I thought. Important things. But she wasn't totally stupid either. Because after she said it she took a quick look at Stan's face, saw the expression on it, and then reached out and touched my shoulder.

"I didn't mean that," she said. "I'm sorry."

She sounded really nice, really sorry, really sincere. Ha! What a liar. She never got to my shoulder though. I wouldn't let her. I never detested anybody so much in my whole life.

Afterward, when old Troy was gone, I wouldn't tell Stan who my friend was, though he asked. You could tell he was sorry about what happened and wanted to make it up somehow, because he sort of hung around looking anxious. And when I got ready to take my dog over to Gareth's house, he wanted to come along. But I wouldn't let him. So far as I was concerned he'd just joined the enemy. In fact, by that time, he was the enemy.

But if you want to know the truth, he looked so guilty and as if he felt so bad and sorry about what happened, I sort of began to enjoy being quiet and distant and scornful, the way I'd been ever since old Troy hit the road. It was mean, because it wasn't really Stan's fault, and I knew it, but all the same, I got a rotten sort of kick out of being that way. He wanted to go down to the newsstand in the village that day and look for a horror comic with me. But I said I didn't want to. Then he offered to take me to Fat George's that night—you could tell he was ready to practically offer me anything—but I wouldn't go. I said I didn't feel like it. I kept him at a distance. I hardly talked to him at all, except to answer "yes" or "no." And when I left to go to Gareth's house, I just took my dog and left. I didn't say good-bye or anything. And as I walked down the beach away from our house, I sort of shuffled along with my head down, like I felt very bad, in case he should be watching from the house.

When I got there, they were both in the house. They'd been playing backgammon. I saw the board set up with red winning, whoever that was. They seemed really glad to see me. And the first moment they saw my dog, they were decent about her, too. Neither of them laughed or said anything to hurt her feelings. They did mention her tail because that was something it was impossible to ignore and they would have been phonies if they hadn't.

"She looks like a very smart dog—and judging by her chest and paws she's going to be quite large when she grows up."

That's what she said. She didn't say my dog was cute or anything. And I was glad. I didn't want her to have to lie or anything. But Gareth thought she was beautiful and said so.

I told them how I found her and that I wasn't allowed to keep her.

And then, before I had to ask, she said, "We could keep her for you, if you'd like us to. Then you can have her back whenever your father will let you keep her."

Which will be never, I thought. But all the same, you notice she didn't say they'd take her? She said they'd keep her, so she'd still be mine. There's a huge, enormous difference between somebody who'd say the first thing and somebody who'd say the second.

"We'll be glad to have her," she said. "I've wanted a dog around the place for a long time."

That's the kind of people they were. They didn't make you ask. And I thought that even if she hadn't wanted a dog, she probably would've taken her anyway, because that's how she was.

Gareth wanted to know her name. He was already petting her broad head and looking lovingly into her yellow eyes.

"She doesn't have one yet," I said. "I can't think of a good one."

She sat on her heels beside my dog and looked intently into her face, half closing her eyes in thought. After a minute she looked at me and said, "How about *Keeper*? It's a good, strong, dignified name for a dog."

La Verne. What an insulting name, I thought. Stan could be so phony sometimes.

"And besides," she said, "I like that name for another reason."

Just that she liked it would have settled it so far as I was concerned. But I asked her what the other reason was anyway.

"Oh," she said, "it's just that Keeper was the name of a dog that belonged to someone I admire. A writer."

She walked over to the bookcase, took down a book, and flipped through the pages until she came to a drawing of a dog that she showed me.

"That's Keeper."

"She'll never look like that," I said.

"Even if she doesn't," she said, "she'll feel better about herself if she has a good name."

She was right. Keeper. I liked it right away. So that's what we named her—Keeper.

I called her by it to see if she liked it. She stood still on her stumpy legs and lifted her broad, ugly face up when she heard it, and as she gave me this really intelligent look and waved her extravagant tail, her eyes glowed red with living fire for an instant and something that had no name moved in smoky gold behind them.

She asked me to stay awhile and eat supper with them. Gareth held his breath—I really did see him stop breathing—until I answered.

I said I could. They didn't care where I was at home. And there wasn't any place else I even remotely wanted to be, so I stayed.

Gareth and Keeper and I went down the beach. We played pirates on the boat. Then we beachcombed awhile and Keeper chased the gulls. After that, we made a fire on the beach, then Gareth's mom came and cooked hot dogs. And then we went back home.

I hated to go. I would've liked to stay with them forever. It was peaceful there. Nothing like the anger or depression we had was in their house. Everything was just quiet and easy. It felt happy there. I sure hated to leave.

When I finally did, though, she walked me to the door. I wanted to tell her I thought Gareth was the nicest little kid and that she was the best looking, most perfect person (except my mom) I ever knew. And that if there was anything in the world I could do for them, anything at all, all they had to do was tell me what it was.

I wanted to say that, but all I managed to say out loud was, "Thanks a lot for keeping my dog and everything."

"That's okay," she said. "We'll take good care of her until you come for her."

As I walked back home I spent the time imagining what I'd do if either of them was in some kind of danger. I ran into a burning building and rescued them. I beat off attackers. I saved them from wild animals and murderers. I pounded to bits people who insulted her. I saved them over and over, in one way or another, all the way back to my house. Sometimes I survived the rescue and sometimes not. It didn't matter. I'd have saved them either way. And it felt better each time I did it.

The house was dark when I came in, but Stan was there. He was sitting in the dark playing *Lulu,* this weird opera he always plays on the stereo when he's in a bad mood.

"Hey, man," he called out when he heard me walk by his room. "Did your friend like the dog?"

"Sure," I said. "She liked her a lot. She thought of a name for her."

"What was it?"

"We named her Keeper," I said.

"She must like Emily Brontë," Stan said.

"What?"

"Keeper," Stan said. "Your friend is obviously a person of some taste and perception."

He looked like he was about to say more and then decided not to. Instead, all he said was, "Well, school tomorrow," sort of briskly, in a way that didn't seem much like him at all—or at least, not much like the way he used to be, the *old* Stan.

I nodded gloomily and left him to listen to his distorted music all by himself. I missed my dog sleeping on my bed. Overnight, I'd already gotten used to her being there, so that I felt lonelier than ever. When I got through missing her, I began to miss my mom, and after my mom, Excalibur. Then I turned over in bed and thought about old Troy and Ivan the Terrible cat and gave up any ideas I had about getting to sleep for a while.

The fog came in. I heard the foghorns over at Cooper's Bay calling to each other a mournful warning. I wished I was far away from there and was somebody else. Anybody but me.

15
Invitations

As mornings go, the next one that rolled around couldn't have been worse. It was Monday, for one thing. There was school. And it was cold and rainy. You would never have known it was June and nearly time for summer vacation. It felt like March. And when I woke up and thought about the day, I wanted to cut school again, like I had on Friday, and then keep on cutting it until summer vacation or maybe forever.

The kitchen was dark and sort of cold when I came into it that morning. It looked just the same as it had when I left it Sunday afternoon. The same two cups that had held coffee in them were still there. I even knew the one old Troy had used because there was a big smear of lipstick on one side of the rim. My mom wore lipstick sometimes, but she never got it all over cups and glasses the way old Troy always did. And Gareth's mom never wore lipstick at all, at least any of the times I'd seen her. She didn't need to.

The same dishes were piled in the sink too. In fact, the only things that weren't still there in the kitchen since the day before were Stan and old Troy. And the only new thing I noticed when I walked in there on Monday morning was a letter. The envelope to it was beside where old Troy had sat. The envelope and letter were both addressed to Dr. Troy Strawbridge and the letterhead said "Stoneygate Military Academy." The letter was from somebody named *John R. Fish, Col. U.S. Army Ret.* It said he was happy to send her the information she had requested and that a transcript of Brady's grades for the last three years would be required. Upon receiving them a personal interview would be arranged for the "young man" and his father. He signed the letter "Truly Yours."

I read that letter more than once. I wasn't surprised. Part of me—the part that kept on saying I wouldn't be able to find my mom or bring her back—had always known I'd be sent away out of everybody's hair. But all the same, I must've been in a kind of shock too, because after I found it, I just stood there and read it over and over, as if I couldn't stop. As if my brain were wrapped in cotton wool, so that I couldn't think too well.

I knew that was what they'd been fighting about when I'd come that Sunday. And I thought, at least, they'd been fighting so they weren't perfectly agreed about it. And Stan had looked all mad and depressed, too.

He was in the living room frowning at a cup of coffee when I finally put the letter down and left the kitchen. He still didn't look like he was in a very good mood, so I heated up a can of chili—Stan and I don't fool too much with cereal or eggs—and poured myself a glass of milk. I kept my mouth shut the whole time except once, when I said as a sort of long shot, "Hey, you know something? I just had a great idea. Why don't we go to San Francisco for a couple of weeks?"

"What?" Stan is one of those guys who, with only two days growth of beard, looked like a bum. He needed a shave that morning. "What are you talking about?"

I gave him this big, false-enthusiastic look.

"We could leave today," I said. "Right now. Come on, how about it? You could see your agent and Joe and Paula and I could go to all the comic book stores. Come on, how about it? What d'ya say? Let's drop everything and *go* for once in our lives. I mean, life is short and—"

"Come off it, Brady," Stan said—he was really in a bad mood. "Just please shut up. I don't feel like talking right now."

So we just sat after that. Stan always reads a book while he drinks his coffee—or does practically anything—so after he said that, he pushed the book he had that day up in front of his eyes in a sort of businesslike way and started to read again. By leaning my head way over to one side I could see what he was reading. It was *Wuthering Heights* by Emily Brontë.

I sat and watched him read. I wondered if I ought to mention Stoneygate. I decided not to. After a while, Stan said, "Aren't you going to eat your chili?"

"Nope." I said, "I'm not hungry."

He didn't look at me. He just reached out with one hand, pulled the bowl in front of him, and began to eat it himself. Then, without lifting his head out of the book, he said, "By the way, I won't be home until late tonight. You need any money?"

What I wanted to say was, I know about Stoneygate, you rat. But all I said was, "If you want to give me five, it'll save me going to my bank to cash a check."

He very nearly smiled at that. He reached in his pocket and handed me a bill. Just before I left the house that morning I went into my room and packed some stuff to take with me. Don't ask me why. I had no plans. All I know is, I took all the money I'd saved, one of the hardcover books Stan had written, and a scarf that belonged to my mom: one she'd worn a lot because it had her favorite flowers—poppies—on it. As I went out the door I heard the opening bars of *Wozzeck*, another opera Stan always played when he was mad or depressed.

School was worse than ever that day. There were long lines of kids getting off the bus in the rain, shoving each other, and yelling stuff at the girls. But, I don't know, it seemed like they did it automatically, because they were supposed to, and not as if their hearts were in it. And as I stood there in the schoolyard and watched, I thought, what was the use of going inside the building at all? There was an algebra quiz I hadn't studied for and some U.S. history homework I hadn't done. What was the use of being there at all? There was no use. So I turned and walked away. I thought I heard Le Moin call after me, but I probably didn't. I kept on walking anyway.

I had no place to go, though. The cave was gone.

Excalibur was gone. My world was empty. I thought how by that time, I might have even not been sure I hadn't imagined the whole thing—about Excalibur, how I might have thought maybe I was crazy or something—except for the shining green-gold mark on the palm of my hand. I looked at it as I walked. It was still there. It glowed softly, like a promise that everything would be better, would be all right.

I doubted it though. My cave was gone. And the dunes, without my mom on them, were just dunes and no place special. I thought of going back home and crawling into pig heaven with some rerun on TV and a bag of barbecue potato chips, but it seemed too lonely without Stan and my dog. And so in the end, I decided to go see how Keeper was and the minute I decided that, I knew it was what I'd had in mind to do all along. Had really planned to do from the minute I'd read that letter that lay on our kitchen floor.

What I really wanted to do was just see Gareth's mom. I hadn't made up my mind how much I'd tell her. I just wanted to be around her that day because I was so lonesome and mixed up about everything. And maybe, I thought, if I talked about some of it, that would be good. And maybe, I thought, if I told her everything about everything—school and old Troy and all—it might be better. But as I walked down the beach toward the Andersen house, I hadn't made up my mind.

I was glad she was alone when I got there. I found her sitting on the front steps with a hammer and a coffee can full of nails beside her. She seemed glad to see me but not surprised.

"Gareth and Keeper are visiting a batch, or is it clutch? A kindle of kittens, that's it (she was like Stan, I thought, the right word was really important to her; she liked words a lot) over at the Corners. Chris Bjornsen invited him. So I'm all alone. I think he'll bring back one to keep." She smiled. "I hope it's a striped one. Are you thirsty or anything?"

I shook my head. I sat down on the step beneath her step. It had stopped raining. The air was mild. It felt good to be outside. Good to be there.

"It might rain again," I said. She glanced at the sky.

"Maybe," she said, "but not hard."

She knew it was Monday morning. Monday morning meant school. Anybody else, any other adult, would've at least asked or tried to be funny about it and have made a joke about cutting school or something. But she didn't. She was perfect. She knew how not to ask something like that better than anyone I ever knew except my mom.

She stuck her hand in the coffee can and pulled out a couple of nails. "I'm looking for a big one to knock into this porch." But after pulling out a few that were too small she laughed and said, "Oh, forget it. Do you feel like going for a walk? Down to Preacher's Rock? I've always wanted to go there. I heard there were moon-stones on that beach. Gareth won't be back until this afternoon. Now's a good chance."

It was fine with me. I like to walk the beach. You never know what you might find. And the beach was so long and wide that it felt like once you started you could go on forever, just walk on it in one direction and never have to turn around or come back.

So we walked on the cold, hard sand in our bare feet with our sneakers in our hands. The sky was all soft and gray, gulls wheeled and screamed over our heads as they begged for bread.

"I should've brought some," she said. The wind tasted like salt. It blew her black hair across her face or out behind her.

As we walked, we talked. At least, I talked. In fact, I ended up telling her all about Stan and old Troy—at least my part of Stan and old Troy. I described Ivan the Terrible in detail. Then I told her about Stoneygate Military Academy and Applegate Village School. I told her how I knew they didn't want me around once they were married. But I didn't mention my mom because I couldn't talk about her to anybody. I was still too disappointed about the way I hadn't been able to get her back. And I didn't tell her about Excalibur because—I don't know why. Maybe because he'd been a secret for so long, I was used to keeping quiet about him, or maybe because I was afraid he belonged to me and nobody else.

But what I did tell her she really listened to, not like some people would who might walk along beside you while you talked and be quiet and all, but who would get distracted by stuff or look at things you passed. She was perfect. She kept her eyes on the sand where we walked and looked very serious but never interrupted me except once when she asked this very intelligent question. And when I'd said everything there was to say and had finished by saying, "I don't know what to do—" she didn't say anything right away. She just kept on walking. You could tell she was thinking, though. And when she finally spoke, it was just so cool. What I mean is, she didn't say anything stupid or useless like, "Oh, Brady, it won't be so bad once you get there," the way most even pretty intelligent people might. She didn't try to comfort me or treat me like a dumb kid either. She didn't pretend to think I ought to like Stoneygate or Applegate. She was honest. All she said was, "Are you sure they'll really send you?"

"Pretty sure," I said. I told her about the letter. We walked a little further down the beach. Then, just as we passed the rock they call the Preacher, she turned her head and looked at me.

"Listen, Brady, any time you want to stay with us overnight or even longer, if it's okay with your dad, we'd like to have you. You're someone we love to have around—like part of the family, you know? And this is a standing invitation for all time. Will you please remember that?"

I looked at her. She looked back at me and what was in her face was—I don't know—something you'd like to keep with you to sort of be able to pull out and look at all the rest of your life. I mean, it was a valuable kind of look. It should've been put in a museum that held all the really good stuff that ever was, it was so nice and beautiful and all.

There were moonstones on the beach when we got there. "The trouble is," I said, "that everybody knows this beach. They always look for moonstones here. It's sort of picked over. But I know a beach that nobody goes to that's got moonstones on it."

"I'd like to go there sometime," she said.

"We can go there any time you want."

I would've done anything for her. And as we walked back home I tried to think of something but nothing seemed good enough.

"I wish there were diamonds on that beach," I said. My ears got hot after I said it, but I was glad I did. She knew what I meant, too.

Because then she said, "I can never forget you saved Gareth's life. But that's not the only reason I said what I did. It's for yourself too. For what you are. And I like moonstones much better than diamonds."

After she said that, we didn't say much. We just walked along together. When we came to this very big log she stopped and sat down.

"Just for one minute," she said. "It's been a long walk. I hope Gareth gets a striped one. Do you like striped cats?"

But I'd been thinking about something I'd wanted to do all along. And this seemed like the right time to do it, so I reached in my pocket.

"Here," I said, "you can have this."

She took it and held it. She looked down at the red and pink poppies on it.

"It was my mom's," I said, "but you can have it. It'll look nice on your hair."

She kept it in her hands as she looked at me. She didn't say anything at all for quite a while. Then, she said, "It's beautiful."

"It's silk."

"Are you sure you want to give it away?"

"Sure," I said, "to you."

She stroked it. Then, slowly and carefully, she knotted it around her neck. The minute she did that, it stopped looking like something familiar that belonged to my mom and turned into something that belonged to her. She looked really neat in it and really beautiful and everything.

Her eyes sparkled like seawater on a bright day. She smiled. She stood up and brushed the sand from the seat of her jeans.

"I've got to go. It's almost time for Gareth to be home."

We didn't talk much on the way back. Once she asked me if I would like to stay and have dinner with them, but I said I couldn't. To tell the truth, I needed to be alone and walk the beach and think.

But before we went in our different directions she said, "Come see us soon. And don't forget, if you need anything, we're here. And don't forget, we're friends forever."

You couldn't say more than that. She was way cool. I would gladly have risked my life for her. But I couldn't say so. It was what I wanted to say. But what I did was, I just sort of looked out over the horizon, as we said good-bye, and mumbled something nobody could hear. She probably didn't even know what I was talking about.

Afterward I walked the beach for a long time. It seemed really important to think the whole thing out, to get it clear in my head. But Excalibur and my mom, old Troy and her cat, Stan and Gareth and Gareth's mom got all jumbled together in my mind. All screamed messages to me in some foreign language I couldn't understand, but that was a matter of life and death to know. And as that happened, I got more and more confused, until I decided it was hopeless to try to figure out anything at all. The more I thought about it, the less I understood. I wondered what would become of me.

Everything I thought was so weird and strange that afternoon that in the end it made me sick. My eyes felt like they were all loose in my head and might explode. I had to sit down on the sand because the bones in my legs got all soft and couldn't hold me up anymore. Something told me that any minute I might have to upchuck on the sand. But more than being sick, I was scared. I didn't know what of. I hadn't figured that out. All I knew was I was more terrified than I'd ever been before in all my life. I was afraid—afraid—afraid.

I put my head down on the sand to make the dizziness go away. I closed my eyes and felt the sand, cold and damp against my cheek. I heard the ocean and thought of the cave and the white beach that wasn't there anymore. And how I called for help the first night I ever saw Excalibur. How I called for help before I crossed the channel through the quicksand.

Then, for the third time, I reached out again with all my mind. I called. And I was answered. It came. It hushed the screaming in my head. It stopped the fear and with a golden stillness that held all the good things I'd ever had—Excalibur, my mom's smile, the dunes—it wrapped me all around.

I kept my eyes shut tight so as not to lose it. And at first there was just the stillness. Then, one by one, thoughts came. But these thoughts were different from the ones I'd had before. They didn't scream in my head. They just sailed in quietly like ships and I knew they weren't my thoughts. They belonged to whatever had answered. It spoke. I listened.

A tree, a thought, a cloud: all these things, it said, and everything else, were inside the stillness. Which was always there. Which was all things to everyone. And helped everyone. But to do that, it took the shape each one needed to see.

For me, Excalibur was the shape it took: He showed me that nothing could be held in prison, made me understand that once he was gone he wouldn't be back, the way my mom wouldn't be back. Because you can't return to something you've outgrown.

And it was Keeper too: ugly as the brute behind Excalibur's mask, with something gold behind her eyes to show me who she was. And it was Gareth's mom, who was beautiful, like Excalibur, and somebody who, like my mom's smile, took me in out of the storm and told me without words that everything was positively all right forever, because somebody loved me.

All those things were connected to each other. And all of them were part of what had answered me, though not all of it, because that had no limits and no end—but just the part of it that belonged only to me: the part it gave me because it loved me.

That was what it said to me. I didn't understand it all, then or now. All I knew was that inside it everything was good and everything was clear. And that when I stepped outside it and was on the beach again, with the sand all damp and cool against my cheek and the gray clouds that moved all soft overhead across the sky, I wasn't scared or sick anymore. Because then I knew that whatever happened to me—Stoneygate or something worse—couldn't hurt me because something was there for me. Like it was there for everybody.

16
Big Deals

As I opened our front door I heard the sound of the Ramones coming from our living room—which is what Stan plays when he's in a good mood.

"It's about time," Stan said when I came into the room. He was sitting under a pile of cassettes and looked fine: better than he had for months and like he felt sociable for a change. I looked at the clock.

"I thought you weren't going to be home till late," I said.

"I changed my plans. Where've you been?"

"Out on the beach," I said.

"Had any dinner?"

"No dinner," I said.

"Want to drive over to Fat George's and get a burger?"

I stared at him. Tired as I was, I pretended to faint with surprise and shock all the same.

"Now?" I said. "You mean *now*? So late and on a school night?"

"I feel mildly euphoric," Stan said. "In fact, I feel like celebrating. It's weird, but there it is."

"Celebrating what?"

Stan grinned, like somebody my age just for the moment, and said, "Troy and I broke up tonight. It's all over. We're through."

I couldn't believe it. I mean, to hear what I heard, coming at the end of the day I'd had and going to Fat George's at the same time was way too good to be true.

I didn't trust it, so I said anxiously, "Are you sure you broke up for good? You won't make up later or anything?"

"It's for good all right," Stan said happily. "What a narrow escape."

We didn't say anything more about it until we were sitting together in one of the big comfortable booths at Fat George's, the way I'd wanted us to on my birthday.

I was eating a Mastodon with everything on it but onions and my second batch of bottomless fries and Stan was eating a cheeseburger, when in the midst of our comfortable chewing he said, "We never really got along."

"Pass the chili sauce," I said.

"You know?" Stan said. "We never did see anything the same way now that I think of it. The difference between us was subtle, but vast. Very vast. What did you want? Salt? Anyway, it was the way she acted about the dog that opened my eyes. I mean, looked at any way, it was cold. And mean. The pound. God. When she said that and I saw the way she looked at you, that was when it all came together in a blinding flash. I saw her in an entirely different light. What I mean is, things I'd never consciously noticed before but must've noticed down somewhere in my mind just all came right up to the surface. Like the way she'd just gone ahead and arranged to send you away without even asking you or me was not only mean, it was stupid. Maybe I'd have seen what she was sooner or later anyway, but maybe it would've been after we were married or something rotten like that. Anyway, as I said, it was the dog that made everything fall into place in my mind, so that I could see the whole thing was hopeless. Hopeless. Awful. We would never have made it as a married couple."

"Not the salt, the chili sauce," I said. "Are you sorry?"

"No, not at all," Stan said. "I feel wonderful."

I could tell he meant it. Because for just one second he stopped smiling from ear to ear and said, "Wow. What a narrow escape. And to think I might have married her after being married to your mom."

He shook his head like somebody who couldn't believe what a fool he was.

We didn't talk too much after that. We just finished our meal by making our own ice cream sundaes with the topping of our choice. Stan's was butterscotch and mine was hot fudge with M&Ms™ sprinkled on top. Then we played a couple of video games and left.

We took the long way home, and as we drove down the dark, narrow road with the pine trees all lined up on either side so that it smelled like Christmas outside the car, Stan began to sing. He did all the verses of "Frankie and Johnny." Then he did Roy Acuff's version of "Pins and Needles in My Heart," complete with the banjo solo, then "The Code of the Mountain." "The Code of the Mountain" is this really neat ballad about two guys who shoot it out away down the backwoods. It's a lonely sounding, haunting song and Stan sang it by request.

You could tell he was happy all right. And full of plans, too. Now that Stoneygate and Ivan the Terrible and all the rest of it was behind us and we were safe—he said— we could start to have some fun. We could do a lot of things: go to San Francisco like I'd said that morning. He'd been thinking about it, he said, and it sounded like a pretty good idea. And we'd go east of the mountains to see the folks and maybe pick apples that fall. There were lots of good things to do now that we were free again.

He gave me this big, happy smile and said, "But the first thing we'll do is get your dog back."

I guess I smiled and nodded when he said that. I'm not sure. I was just so relaxed, so relieved that everything I'd been so worried about was over—I could barely keep my eyes open. All I could think of was my bed upstairs and my pillow that molts like a chicken unless you keep two pillowslips on it.

The next day, as soon as school was over, Stan and I walked over to get my dog. Gareth's mom answered the door. She was in her bare feet, so she couldn't have been going anyplace special. But all the same, she looked like she ought to be. It was the shirt she wore. It was made out of some soft material that was the color of seaweed and showed how her eyes were the color of beach glass. It made her look beautiful and strange, like some kind of water witch or something.

It was sort of awkward at first. I told her who Stan was and everything. Then she smiled at him and I wished she hadn't, because he did nothing but embarrass me after that. I mean, after she smiled at him, he did everything wrong: he hardly smiled himself, when his smile is one of the best things about him and sort of cancels out the tiny little bald spot he's getting. He hardly spoke either, and Stan without words is not Stan at all. And what he did do he did too much of, which was to stare at her and look all ignorant, like he'd forgotten what we were even there for. Gareth wasn't around to help matters any either, so finally I was the one who had to say why we'd come. Stan was completely out of it.

She looked upset when I mentioned Keeper.

"Keeper," she said. "Keeper isn't here. I'm afraid she's disappeared. She just left the house yesterday. We spent all day on the beach calling and looking for her, but we didn't find her. And she's not at any of the animal shelters because we walked over to Bjornsen's and called. We were going to tell you about it if we didn't find her today. We hoped, that is, we waited in case we found her or heard something. But she doesn't seem to be anywhere. She seems to have vanished into thin air. I'm sorry, Brady. We feel bad about it."

You could tell she really was sorry, too.

"That's okay," I said. "It isn't your fault."

"Maybe we'll find her," she said. "Maybe she'll turn up."

"Maybe," I said.

I knew she wouldn't though. Because what had Keeper been but just another form of Excalibur? And as Keeper, she had served her purpose. There was no more need for her.

There isn't a lot more to tell. It's probably pretty obvious what happened with Stan and Gareth's mom. I mean, you could say it was something that had to happen once they met and everything. It didn't take too long either. They were married as fast as Stan could get it together once she said it would be okay.

I never told anybody about Excalibur. I still think of him a lot and sort of wait to see him again. I don't know what shape he'll take next time because I don't know what kind of trouble I'll be in to make me need him. I don't even have any solid guarantee he'll be back for sure to help me. But he said he would. And the green-gold mark he left me is still in the palm of my hand, so I think he will. I know he will.

DATE DUE
